Readers love the ~~Carlisle Cops~~
series by ANDREW GREY

Fire and Water

"Yes, I enjoyed every minute of this sweet and lovable comfort read."
—Prism Book Alliance

"All of Andrew Grey's books are good, but I think I just found a new favorite!"
—Love Bytes Reviews

Fire and Ice

"I am continually amazed with Grey's imagination. He constantly comes up with fresh new story ideas to keep his readers entertained and chomping at the bit for the next story."
—TTC Books and More

"This is a story that touches the heart as well as heats the blood. I hope we see more of the Carlisle Cops in the future!"
—House of Millar

Fire and Rain

"Andrew Grey continues to amaze me with his ability to write stories that will pull at your heartstrings and draw you into the world in which the characters live."
—Gay Book Reviews

"...one of my favorite books he's written.... a love story, a slow burn that leaves you with no doubt the couple will make it through anything life throws their way."
—Two Chicks Obsessed with Books and Eye Candy

Published by DREAMSPINNER PRESS
www.dreamspinnerpress.com

By ANDREW GREY (CONT.)

THE BULLRIDERS
A Wild Ride • A Daring Ride • A Courageous Ride

BY FIRE
Redemption by Fire • Strengthened by Fire • Burnished by Fire • Heat
Under Fire

CARLISLE COPS
Fire and Water
Fire and Ice
Fire and Rain
Fire and Snow

CHEMISTRY
Organic Chemistry • Biochemistry • Electrochemistry

GOOD FIGHT
The Good Fight • The Fight Within • The Fight for Identity • Takoda
and Horse

LAS VEGAS ESCORTS
The Price • The Gift

LOVE MEANS…
Love Means… No Shame • Love Means… Courage
Love Means… No Boundaries
Love Means… Freedom • Love Means … No Fear
Love Means… Healing
Love Means… Family • Love Means… Renewal • Love Means… No
Limits
Love Means… Patience • Love Means… Endurance

SENSES
Love Comes Silently • Love Comes in Darkness
Love Comes Home • Love Comes Around
Love Comes Unheard • Love Comes to Light

Published by DREAMSPINNER PRESS
www.dreamspinnerpress.com

Published by DREAMSPINNER PRESS
www.dreamspinnerpress.com

FIRE AND *Snow*

ANDREW GREY

DREAMSPINNER PRESS

Published by
DREAMSPINNER PRESS

5032 Capital Circle SW, Suite 2, PMB# 279, Tallahassee, FL 32305-7886 USA
www.dreamspinnerpress.com

Fire and Snow
© 2016 Andrew Grey.

Cover Art
© 2016 L.C. Chase.
http://www.lcchase.com
Cover content is for illustrative purposes only and any person depicted on the cover is a model.

ISBN: 978-1-63477-327-0
Digital ISBN: 978-1-63477-328-7
Library of Congress Control Number: 2016901406
Published May 2016
v. 1.0

Printed in the United States of America
∞
This paper meets the requirements of
ANSI/NISO Z39.48-1992 (Permanence of Paper).

To Dominic, for everything he does for me, and for Jane, an amazing editor who taught me a great deal. I will miss you!

CHAPTER
One

"HEADING OUT on patrol?" Red asked as JD Burnside stopped to grab his coat and hat before going outside. Red looked him over and shook his head. "Here. You're going to need these gloves, and put on an extra pair of socks."

"It's only November...," JD said, getting a little worried.

"Maybe, but the wind will go right through you, and they have you on foot patrol in the square. That cold concrete is going to leach the heat right out through your shoes unless you have something extra on."

JD sighed and sat back down in the locker room, going through his things until he came up with a second pair of socks. He slipped off his boots and pulled them on. Instantly his feet began to sweat, but he ignored it and pulled on his now-tight boots. "Is there anything else I should know?"

"Be sure to keep your citation book handy. Fallfest is just winding down, and everyone should be going home, but that also means the heavy-duty revelers will take it into the bars, so be on the lookout for people weaving and bobbing. We don't want them driving home."

"Is that why I'm supposed to be outside in god-awful weather like this instead of tucked in a nice warm patrol car like a regular person?" At least the patrol car would have heat. JD had not gotten used to the weather up in Central Pennsylvania, and he was beginning to realize that his first winter here was going to be hard as hell to get through.

"We always have someone visible to deter drunk driving. I did it two years ago, and Carter had the glorious honor last year. It's only for a day, and all you need to do is keep yourself warm and your eyes open.

1

Everyone will empty out in three or four hours, and then you can come on back and grab a patrol car. These are always interesting evenings."

"Yeah?" JD inquired as he got to his feet.

Red grinned. "A few years ago, they had this cow parade thing where artists decorated fiberglass cows and they put them around the area. There were four of them in town, and one was on the square. That year we had someone decide it was a bull and that he was going to ride it… buck naked in the middle of town." Red began to laugh. "By the time we got to him, he'd turned half-blue and all his friends were getting ready to take their turn. We stopped them before the entire crowd turned into a streak-fest."

"What happened to the naked guy?"

"We hauled him away for indecent exposure, and he got a fine. The thing is, this may be a small town, but we have some crazies when they drink. So keep an eye out and call if you see anything. I'll be around and will stop by to check on you."

JD thanked Red for his help and the story, which had brightened his mood a little. He made sure he had everything and slammed his locker closed before leaving the station and heading out through town toward the square.

He was a block away from the square. When he arrived, he glanced up at the clock tower on the old courthouse to check the time.

"Assault in progress, courthouse common" came through his radio.

JD responded and raced forward, heart pounding. He rounded the courthouse and saw a group of three college students crowded around one of the benches.

"What the hell do you think you're doing, old man?" one of the boys was yelling, the sound carrying through the square. The others yelled as well.

"What's going on?" JD projected in his best police voice. The students backed away, hands exposed, which JD liked. At least they didn't seem to be a threat to him.

"This old guy was about to take a leak on the veterans' memorial," said the kid who'd been doing the yelling. "We sat him down and were trying to talk to him, but he tried to hit Hooper here." He took a further step back and gave JD room. A man in his late sixties, if JD had to guess, sat on the bench, shaking like a leaf. The front of his pants was wet, and he smelled. When JD touched him, the man felt cold, and he continued to shiver. JD tried more than once to get the man to look at him, and when he finally did, his eyes were vacant and half-lidded.

"I need an ambulance on High Street next to the old courthouse," JD called in. The man continued to shiver and shake. This wasn't just from the cold. The scent of alcohol permeated even the mess he'd made of himself. The man needed help.

"Is he going to be all right?" Hooper asked. "We didn't hurt him or anything. He was going to take a leak right there on the memorial, and we tried to stop him and help him sit down, but he swung at me and nearly fell." The kid seemed upset. His eyes were as big as saucers.

"Did he hit you?" JD asked.

"No. He was too slow. But David here, the big idiot, started yelling, and that must have been what you heard."

"How much have you had to drink?" JD asked David.

"Enough to know I won't be driving," David answered with blinky eyes.

"None of you had better," JD advised.

"I'm their ride," Hooper said. "I hate the taste of the stuff, so they buy me food and Cokes, and I drive the idiots home." One of Hooper's friends bumped him on the shoulder.

JD turned back to the old man, who was rocking slightly from side to side. JD tried to get his name, but he was becoming more and more unresponsive. JD got the students' information and sent them on their way. He could check with them if he needed to, but what they'd said rang true.

There must have been plenty of calls already, but an ambulance finally arrived and they got the man settled into it. He didn't have any identification on him. JD made sure to get the information he could, and then the EMTs took the man to the hospital.

At least during that excitement he hadn't had a chance to be cold. Once the ambulance pulled away, the square turned quiet. Dry leaves rustled in the trees, and wisps flashed in the lights that lit the side of the old courthouse. JD shivered when he realized those wisps were snow. God, he was going to freeze to death here.

JD pushed that thought aside and walked around the square, then along the side streets, watching for trouble. He passed a few people still huddled on the benches, but he figured they'd soon give up and head on home.

Now that the streets were no longer blocked off for the festival, traffic continued flowing through the main intersection, as it usually did. JD returned to the intersection, crossed High Street and then Hanover, then continued around to the narrow side street that ran next to one of the churches on the square. He hated that street. It wasn't well lit and there were plenty of shadows.

He peered down to check for movement and was preparing to move on when Red pulled up in a patrol car. JD opened the passenger door and got inside.

"I saw you heading this way and thought we could take a ride for a while," Red said.

JD was eternally grateful as he soaked up the heat inside the car. "I hate that street."

"We all do. The chief is going to demand a streetlight. The church has been fighting it because they say it will mess up the light coming in from the stained-glass windows or something. But lately it's become a real hazard." Red put the car in gear and made the turn, slowly rolling down the street.

At the slight bend, two figures raced out of a corner and took off down the street toward the church's back parking lot. Red flipped on his lights while JD jumped out and took off on foot. Red raced past him to try to head the men off.

JD was fast. He had run track in high school and college, and no street punk was going to outrun him. He pounded the pavement, feet racing. One of the men dodged and got away once, but when he tried it again, JD was ready and grabbed the back of his coat, yanking the man to a stop.

He fell to the ground and rolled. JD stayed on his feet, and when the man stopped rolling, JD knelt and placed his knee on his back.

"I wasn't doing nothing," the man protested.

"Yeah, I'm sure," JD said as Red pulled up.

"The other one got away," Red said angrily.

4

"This one was throwing things out of his pocket as he ran," JD said, pointing back the way they'd come.

"Oh man. You going to try to pin shit on me now?" the man asked as he shifted on the ground.

JD cuffed him and made sure he was secure. "Nope. I'm going to make sure you get what you've got coming to you." JD watched as Red carefully photographed and tagged what had been thrown aside. The law had been the family profession for generations, so JD had decided to become a police officer. But once he'd started down the path, he'd discovered a love of fair play, protecting others, and enforcing the law. Maybe it was genetic? He wasn't sure.

Other sirens sounded, and soon two more cars joined them, bathing JD and the suspect in headlights.

"What have we here?" Aaron Cloud, one of the detectives, asked as he got out of his car.

"Cocaine, by the looks of it," Red answered. "Enough of it that he's going to be doing some long, hard time."

"That ain't mine," the suspect said.

JD shook his head. "I saw him throwing it out of his pockets, with his bare hands, as I chased him. It was his. His prints will be on the bags." The guy must be an idiot.

"Go ahead and read him his rights. We'll take him down to the station."

"There was another man with him," Red said. "JD here jumped out of the car when we saw him, took off like a shot, and got this guy. I followed the other man, but he ran between the houses over there and disappeared across High Street."

"We'll find out who he was," Aaron said, looking down at the suspect. "Won't we?" The menacing tone Aaron used had the guy shaking a little. JD knew it was an act. Detective Cloud was a "by the book" kind of guy, but if he hadn't been a police officer, he could have had a career in Hollywood.

Aaron took custody of the suspect, and JD helped Red confirm they had found everything that had been thrown by their suspect before driving to the station.

"I don't think I've ever been so grateful for a drug bust in my life," JD said as they rode, the wipers swishing back and forth to wipe the falling snow from the windshield.

They passed the square slowly. JD turned when he saw movement. A man stood up from one of the benches and slowly walked away. "Are there always people on those benches? They have to be freezing in this weather."

"Yeah. People sit there all day long. They have their favorite spots, and heaven help anyone who tries to take it. Mostly people just pass them by and don't really notice them." Red made the turn and continued to the station. JD pulled his mind away from the bench sitters back to the report he was going to have to help write.

At least the station was warm. JD went to his desk and got to work putting together his statement of events.

"You did good," Red told him as he passed. "Though I don't recommend jumping out of moving cars every day."

"Did we get any information out of him?" JD asked.

"Aaron is leaning on him pretty hard. He'll probably lawyer up pretty soon, but he says the other guy was just a customer," Red explained, which was what JD had figured. At least they got the dealer this time. Usually it was the other way around. "Did you send in your statement?"

JD nodded and stood up. It was time for him to go back out on patrol. At least this time of night he'd have a vehicle. "I'll head out with you." Red walked him to the parking lot, and they got in their respective cars. "Stay safe."

"You too." JD started the engine, then pulled out of the lot. He drove through town and turned into the same side street he and Red had gone down earlier. It was empty this time, and he continued on.

The snow was getting heavier, and he drove carefully as visibility got worse and the streets more slippery. Toward the end of his shift, he made one last tour of town. He passed the square and saw a single figure on one of the benches in the courthouse square. JD knew there was nothing wrong with sitting on the bench, but it was after eleven and cold as hell. He pulled to the side of the street and got out, then walked up to the man.

He was hunched and curled into his coat, arms wrapped around himself, chin to his chest.

"Sir, are you all right?"

The man looked up and then lowered his gaze once again, saying nothing.

"Sir, is something wrong? It's way too late and too cold to be out here. You should head on home."

"I'm fine. Doesn't matter, anyway. No one cares." He lowered his gaze once again and continued sitting where he was.

"You'll be a lot warmer and safer if you go home." JD was becoming concerned. "I can help if you like? Can you tell me where you live?"

"Of course I can. But it doesn't matter. Nothing matters." He got to his feet. He seemed steady enough. "People are crap, you know that? Everyone takes advantage of everyone else, and no one gives a crap about it." He took a few steps, weaving slightly, and then he straightened up and headed off toward the courthouse. "No one cares about anything or anyone."

"Do you need some help?" JD asked.

"No. There's nothing you can do." He walked off and JD watched him go. Something wasn't right, but he was cold and the guy seemed harmless enough. JD went back to his car and slowly drove down the road. He saw where the man turned, and then watched as he went inside one of the apartment buildings in the first block of Pomfret.

His phone rang, so JD pulled to a stop before answering it. "You heading back to the station?" Red asked.

"Yeah." He checked the time.

"Terry is going to meet me at Applebee's. They're still open, and we can get something to eat." Red had been nice enough to befriend him when he'd joined the force six months earlier.

"Sounds good. Let me get back and finish up. I'll meet you there."

JD drove back to the station, checked in, and then left. The snow barely covered the ground, but it was enough to make him itchier about driving. He knew people here didn't think too much about a little snow, but he'd rarely driven in it back home. As he clutched the wheel, he tried to remember the last time he'd actually driven in snow. It must have been four or five years ago.

JD approached Hanover Street and saw a hunched figure walking back toward the square. JD knew he was off duty, but he turned left instead of right anyway. He watched as the man went back to the same bench and sat down. There was something very wrong.

JD pulled off the road, then got out and jogged across the street to where the man sat. "I thought you'd gone home," JD said gently.

"This is my bench. I like it here."

"Dude, it's really cold, and you're going to get sick." JD helped him to his feet. "It's also really late. You need to get home where it's safe and warm." He hoped the guy wasn't sick, but he couldn't leave him out in this weather. "When was the last time you ate?"

The man shrugged. JD looked at his arm, checking for a medical bracelet. He'd had a friend who acted like this sometimes, a little loopy and strange. He'd been diabetic, and when his blood sugar got wacky, he'd act really out of it. "Why don't you come with me, and I'll see about getting you something to eat."

"Okay," the man agreed, and JD helped him walk across the street. He got him into the car, wondering what Red was going to think when he showed up with a stranger. The guy sat quietly, lightly fidgeting with his hands as JD drove to the edge of town and pulled into the restaurant parking lot.

"Let's get you something to eat, and then maybe you'll feel better." JD had committed himself now. He'd crossed a line between officer and public a long time ago—and if this turned out badly, he could be in a hell of a lot of trouble—but something told him the guy wasn't dangerous, just a little confused.

He parked and they got out, the man following docilely.

Red met him at the restaurant door, staring quizzically. "Who's this?"

"He's…." Shit, how was he going to explain this? "A guy who needs some help."

Red turned slightly, looking at JD like he'd truly lost his mind. "Is that some Southern thing?" Red asked.

"It's a human thing," JD answered.

Red rolled his eyes, pulling open the door to the restaurant. "Terry got us a booth already," he said, leading them toward the corner. Terry stood in all his toned swimmer glory, smiling brightly in his snug-fitting clothes. JD had met Red's partner only a few times before, but his shirts always seemed perfectly tight and his pants hugged his legs just so. JD did his best not to look too closely or ogle the man, but it was dang hard. "You remember JD," Red said.

"Of course. How are you, JD?" Terry said. "And this is…?"

"Fisher Moreland," the man answered in a clear voice.

"Glad you could join us," Terry added, shaking his hand and then sliding into the booth. Red sat next to him, and JD motioned for Fisher to take a seat before sliding in after him.

"How was your shift?" Terry asked.

"Interesting," Red said. "JD here tackled a dealer as he tried to run away." Red handed out menus. "It was something to see. He flew after the guy and brought him down with a grab. It was beautiful."

"I'm just glad it worked out," JD said, letting Red do most of the talking. The server approached and they ordered drinks. When Fisher didn't respond, JD ordered him a Coke, hoping the sugar was what he needed. She left and they went back to talking, but JD kept an eye on Fisher, who was once again huddling down into his coat. When the drinks arrived, Fisher shakily put a straw into the soda and drank. JD shared looks with the others, but he didn't say anything about it. He was starting to think he should have called an ambulance to help the guy, and that this was a huge mistake.

"Are you getting used to this cold?" Terry asked JD.

"God, no." A chill ran through him at the thought. "I had no idea it could get so cold, and it's only November."

"Yeah. You have some cold months ahead, but hopefully it won't be as bad as last year. It was frigid for most of January."

"Are you ready to order?" the server asked as she came up to the table, and JD turned to Fisher.

"Chicken wings, please," Fisher said softly. He'd drained the soda, and she took the glass to refill it. JD ordered a burger, and Terry got a salad with the dressing on the side. Red, on the other hand, ordered enough food to feed an army, and JD had no doubt he'd eat it all. Red was a man who loved his food.

"What do you do, Fisher?" Terry asked as the server brought back Fisher's refilled glass.

"I work as a dispatcher at one of the warehouses in that logistics complex out off I-81," Fisher answered. "I'm one of the guys who makes sure the trucks have a place to dock and then tells them where to unload or load up when we're shipping out." He seemed more lucid and his eyes less vacant.

"Do you have family in town?" JD asked.

"Yeah. My family has been here for a long time. But I don't see them very much." He drank some more and the server brought a basket of chicken wings in some goopy sauce along with a plate. Fisher picked up a wing, put it on the plate, and then began to cut it apart with a knife and fork. He ate carefully and slowly, taking apart each wing in the same exacting manner.

"Are they good?" JD asked. Fisher nodded, continuing to eat. As he did, he got more animated, and relief welled in JD that he'd been right and Fisher had needed something to eat.

"Are you all police officers?" Fisher asked once he'd eaten half the wings and the rest of their food had been delivered by the server.

"JD and Red are," Terry said. "I work as a lifeguard and swim instructor at the Y."

"Terry is going to the Olympics," Red said. "He's been training for a long time, and he's going to do well." Red was obviously proud of his partner.

"I saw an article about you in the paper a few months ago. I didn't recognize you. That's so cool." He seemed happy now as he returned to his wings. JD dug into his burger, noticing that Fisher's eyes were bright and clear now.

"Was there any other excitement?" Terry asked as he took a bite of his burger.

"Just an old man who needed some help at the square. He seemed to be having some sort of episode, and I got an ambulance for him. Other than that, it was an exercise in keeping warm. How about you, Red?"

"Nothing. The bars kept us busy, and I convinced some guys to call a cab rather than try to drive. It's what we do after things like this. People drink and then don't make the best decisions, and I'd rather guide them to good ones than arrive at an accident or make a drunk-driving arrest."

"Have you been a police officer long?" Fisher asked JD.

"A couple of years. I went to the academy in South Carolina and got my first job in my hometown there. But things didn't work out too well, and I started looking for a new job. Since I was willing to move, a recruiter got me in touch with the chief here. I never intended to move someplace cold, but the town is pretty nice." He left it at that. There was no reason to go into the whole story about why he'd had to leave his home. Things were different here, and he was grateful for it. "People here have been supportive." JD felt Fisher tense next to him. He turned slightly, but Fisher had returned to eating and the moment passed.

"What do you do for fun?" Red asked Fisher.

"I like researching antiques, and I like to cook," Fisher answered, setting down his knife and fork.

"What's your favorite dish to make?" Terry asked.

"I like to bake bread," Fisher said with energy. "Mixing the dough and then letting it rise, working and kneading it, then baking it, filling the apartment with the scent that means home and warmth. There's nothing better. I bake all my own from scratch, and when I don't have enough time, I have this recipe for a dutch-oven bread that you don't knead. It's really simple and rustic with a great texture. I love making it this time of year. It's a great winter bread."

"I love sourdough," JD said.

Fisher bounced on the seat. "I have a starter that I got years ago. I have to feed it every so often, and I love to use it to make rolls. They have this great crispy crust and that slightly sour flavor that mixes well with sweet melted butter."

JD still had food on his plate, but compared to what Fisher was describing, the burger and fries had lost some of their appeal. Fisher was grinning with excitement, and JD loved that look. He had a slight gap between his teeth, but it was perfect and added to Fisher's smile the same way the little lines that reached toward his eyes gave Fisher's face warmth and character.

"What about you, JD?" Terry inquired. "You have something you like to do for fun?"

"I used to go hunting with my dad. That was our thing. Each fall we'd go out in the woods, just him and me. Between the two of us, we'd get a deer. Bagging something was no big deal. It was spending time together that was the real fun. We'd pack up a tent and spend three or four days tramping through the woods, eating crap my mother would never let us eat at home and having a good time. My sister decided one year that she wanted to go along. My mother forced my dad to take her, and he agreed, just to keep peace in the family."

"How did that work?" Fisher asked.

"We had to take a second tent that my dad and I had to put up for her. Rachel was bored the entire time and kept wanting us to do things to entertain her. Either that or we'd go sit in the blind, and then she'd whine about how there was nothing to do."

"That doesn't sound like fun," Terry commented between bites.

"It wasn't. I was ready to kill her after a day, and I could tell my dad was at his wit's end. After two days, he said we were going to go home because he couldn't take any more. So that morning, we got up and went out for a few hours before packing up." JD looked all around the table. "We were sitting in our blinds. I could see Dad. He was strung tight, and he'd just said through the walkie-talkie that we'd give it another half hour and then go home. Then minutes later a shot rang through the woods, followed by a high-pitched bellow that sent chills through me. I honestly thought my sister had shot herself. Dad and I climbed down and raced toward the sound. We found Rachel standing over this huge buck. Had to be ten points. He was massive, and she was grinning like an idiot." JD paused. "All she said was 'Now I get hunting.' The look in her eyes was feral."

"Does she still go?"

"Every year, and she's always the one who gets the big one. It's like she's deer-nip. They come right to her." JD motioned with his hands, and the others all laughed. "Dad just shakes his head whenever anyone brings it up."

"So is Rachel an outdoor kind of girl?" Fisher asked.

JD laughed. "Hell no. She's this prim and proper Southern belle who loves dresses, looking perfect, and twisting the boys around her little finger, but once a year she and my dad head to the woods in jeans, boots, and flannel. Whoever she marries had better be able to look amazing in a tuxedo and be willing to keep up with her when hunting season comes around." They all laughed. "Oh, and he'll have to be the one to drag whatever she bags out of the woods, because she'll shoot it, but she isn't about to dress or drag it. She'd mess up her nails."

"What did your dad say to that?" Red asked.

"He was so shocked when she shot the buck, he found himself agreeing to anything. Especially after she looked him square in the eye and said that she shot it, and her job was done. She went back to camp and waited while we brought the deer. The thing was, she didn't even make lunch, which I suppose was a small blessing because Rachel can't cook worth a damn. It's a good thing she's pretty and determined."

"Dang. My sisters are cheerleaders," Fisher said. "At least they were the last time I talked to them. And my younger brother is pretty much perfect." Fisher finished eating the wings, and when the server returned he asked for a glass of ice water. He seemed like a very different person from the guy JD had met at the square. JD was still trying to figure Fisher out.

Red's plate was empty, and he sat back with a yawn.

"I know. We need to get you home soon," Terry said softly.

"I hate second shift. First is great, even third is okay, but second is always so hard. The days seem so out of whack. Thankfully I'm up for promotion, and with the job comes permanent first shift, so I'm really looking forward to that."

"So am I," Terry said, leaning close to Red and gently patting his stomach. "It'll be nice to have you working close to the same hours I do."

"Do you have plans after the Olympics?" Fisher asked Terry. "Will you still compete?"

"No. Win or lose, after the competition, I'm done. I love to swim, but we've talked about it, and after we get back from Rio, I'm going to finish school and get a degree in physiology so I can train other athletes. I'd like to be able to train the next generation of swimmers. But all that hinges on the games. If I win, I'll have a lot of credibility and might be able to work that into something lucrative while the publicity holds. Who knows? I'm happy to be going and competing. That alone is a dream come true."

Terry yawned as JD finished up his burger. It was past midnight, and the restaurant was closing. The server brought their checks, and JD paid for his and Fisher's meals. Then they all got up and began pulling on coats.

"I'll see you tomorrow afternoon," Red said as he hugged JD. Terry did the same to him and then to Fisher, who seemed ill at ease at first and then broke into a smile. Maybe he wasn't used to being hugged.

They left the restaurant and went to their cars. The snow had stopped, but the cars and grass were covered in a dusting of white. The pavement was wet and felt a little slippery. JD walked carefully and unlocked the car, letting Fisher get inside.

"Thank you for the food and the company," Fisher said as JD backed out of the space. "It isn't often that a stranger is kind to someone else." The tone of his voice told JD there was a lot more being said than was there in the words. He suspected quite strongly that Fisher was a lonely man, and he was glad he'd been able to help him. "It was what I think I needed. Your friends are very nice."

"They are. Moving to a strange town and a completely different area of the country has taken a lot of adjustment." Not that he had a great deal of choice in the matter.

"I've lived here all my life, and you have more friends than I do." Fisher shifted from watching out the windows as JD turned onto Pomfret. He pulled up at the curb, and Fisher got out of the car. "Thank you again. I really appreciate it." He closed the car door and hurried to the door of the building, then disappeared inside.

JD pulled away and drove the few blocks to his small rented house on South Street. He hadn't meant to get a house, but after looking around at tiny apartments, he'd found the house. It needed some love, but the rent was right. The landlord, who was older and had owned the house for decades, had agreed that any work JD did could be taken off the rent, and he liked the idea of a police officer living there, so JD had moved in and had already done a lot of work on the place.

He unlocked the front door and stepped into the house, which felt more and more like home every day. His furniture had been carefully gathered from consignment and secondhand stores. He'd worked on each piece to make it his. His one splurge was the flat-screen television that sat on the entertainment cabinet in the living room. Other than that, he'd stayed very close to budget. It wasn't as though he had anyone to back him up, not anymore.

JD put his keys on the table by the door and lugged his bag of gear toward the back of the house. He locked up his weapon and threw a load of laundry into the washer before flopping down into his favorite chair in the living room and turning on the television. He didn't bother turning on any lights. He leaned back to get comfortable and managed to fall asleep in the chair before he could really get interested in whatever had been on television.

He woke hours later with Fisher's face and smile on his mind. Something about him got to JD. Maybe it was the loneliness that seemed ever present in his eyes, a feeling JD tried to cover up but knew quite well. He had people he knew from work—friends, even, like Terry and Red—but there was no one here, not like back home, where there were people he'd known since he was a kid running through the sprinklers on a hot day, yelling and carrying on. Carlisle held none of that kind of history for him. Not that it had counted for much in the end.

With a sigh, JD pushed himself out of the chair, turned off the television, and went upstairs to bed. Tomorrow was going to be a long day; he felt it deep down.

BEING A cop often meant hard work and days that didn't seem to end, but his phone rang at eight in the morning, way too early. He snatched it off the dresser, expecting it to be work calling him in. "Hello," he said, trying to sound groggy and pitiful.

"Jefferson Davis, it's your mother." She always managed to sound as though she were snapping orders. "Your aunt died this morning. I thought I should call and let you know. Though we don't expect you to come back for the funeral, you might send flowers."

JD was at a loss for words. His Aunt Lillibeth had been the one person in the family who hadn't turned her back on him. This was just another reminder that he was truly alone, and whatever life he thought he'd once had was gone.

The sound his mother made was something no lady should ever make; at least his aunt would have said so. "Jefferson Davis, the family is just beginning to put this whole… disgraceful… display behind us." Each word seemed to be painful for her. He was her son, and his mother should have been standing behind him, as the rest of the people he'd been close to should have, but no. "It's best if you send flowers to show your respect and that you remember her, but stay away. Some distance and time will help everyone heal and move on."

"Meaning it would be best for you," JD pressed. "Don't lie to me, Mother. You don't want me to come to my aunt's funeral because you're afraid of what those bitches around town will be saying about me. Just admit the truth. You're a coward." He'd had more than enough of his mother's hypocrisy.

"Fine. Think of me what you will. Lord knows I gave up a lot for my children, and heaven forbid I should have some peace of mind and friends in my old age. I went through a great deal to take care of you and your sister while your father worked all those hours at the office and did God knows what with his secretaries."

"I see your ability to reach the heights of drama isn't affected by Aunt Lillibeth's death."

"Don't be flip with me. I've had about all I can take right now with your aunt's death and your father deciding he's going to retire. Lord, what am I going to do with him around the house every day?"

"Stop screwing your tennis instructor?" JD asked.

"Don't be crass," she snapped. "How dare you insinuate that I'm having an affair?" The indignation in her voice told him that his joke had probably come closer to the truth than he'd thought.

"All right, Mother. You're as pure as the driven snow and as gentle and kind as a lamb." He was getting fed up with this conversation.

"There's no need for sarcasm."

"Just send me the info about when the funeral will be, and I'll decide what I want to do," JD insisted. He might as well let his mother dangle in the wind for a while. Let her wonder if he was willing to come down to Charleston and start the rumors and talk all over again. The truth was that he wasn't looking forward to it, and that Aunt Lillibeth wouldn't have wanted it either. She'd been the one to advise him to leave and make a life somewhere else, where he could be himself.

"Fine. You'll do what you like," she huffed. "There isn't anything I can do about it, but at least think of what you'll put your family through."

"Fine, Mom. Is that all you called for? You told me the news and decided to rub salt into an open wound. Are you happy now?" JD got out of bed and pulled on a pair of sweats against the chill. He needed to clean up and knew he wouldn't go back to sleep, not after his mother's call. "If you're done piling on the guilt, I'm going to go now." She was his mother, but JD was coming to realize he really didn't like her much.

"I was just making sure you knew what happened." An uncomfortable silence settled over the connection.

"If there's nothing else, I'm going to go. I worked late last night, and—"

"I don't know how you can do that. A policeman, working with all those criminals. If you wanted to work in the law, you should have become a lawyer. You could have been very successful, but now…." The tsking sound was more than JD could take.

"Good-bye, Mom," JD said and ended the call. If he remained on the line, he was going to get angry and even more hurt. His aunt's passing wasn't unexpected. She'd been ill for some time with a heart condition and had been declining rapidly for the past six months. Still, it hurt that his mother had felt the need to call not only to tell him, but to make sure he didn't come home. The perfect way to start the day: a heaping helping of loathing mixed with a huge dollop of guilt.

JD sighed and tossed his phone on the bed, then retrieved it and fanned through the contacts for someone he could call to talk to about his aunt. But as he thumbed through, he realized, even with all the names, those doors were closed to him now. He placed the phone on the nightstand and turned away from it. Thank goodness he had to go to work. At least there he'd be around people who were less toxic than his own family. Hell, even the people he arrested were less poisonous to his soul than his own fucking family.

With a sigh, JD went into the bathroom. He brushed his teeth well, remembering the number of times his mother had told him to brush his teeth, always with a reminder of exactly how much, to the penny, they'd paid for him to have braces. JD ground his teeth at the thought and nearly swallowed a mouthful of toothpaste, which reminded him he needed to get to the store to get something better than the awful stuff he was using. Maybe he could find something cinnamon flavored. Spitting into the sink, he rinsed his mouth, shaved, and started the shower. Once he was done, he figured he'd do his errands before starting his shift.

CHAPTER
Two

FISHER MORELAND got out of bed and checked the clock. Thankfully his body had awakened him only fifteen minutes after the time his alarm should have gone off. That still meant he had to hurry or he was going to be late for work, which was a huge no-no. He punched a clock, so being one minute late was noticed and would be reflected in his evaluation.

Fisher rushed to the bathroom and shaved before jumping into the shower. His pace made him jittery. He hated running late—it upset everything about his day and meant he had to skip something in his morning routine, and that always left him wondering what he'd forgotten and left him looking over his shoulder.

Once he'd showered, Fisher wrapped a towel around his skinny waist and pulled open the medicine cabinet. He pulled out the weekly pill container he set up each Sunday and opened it, groaning softly when he realized today was Sunday and his pills for Saturday were sitting in their slot. At least that explained the blues that had descended over him and the roller coaster he'd been on. It also accounted for the few hours he couldn't remember from last evening. Oh, he remembered the restaurant with JD, Red, and Terry, and the food, the talking, the lightheartedness. But pretty much all he remembered about the hours before that was being cold and alone. The feeling stayed with him even if the exact memories of what happened were lost.

Fisher doled out his upcoming week of medications into their slots, then took his Sunday pills from the container, placed them in his palm, and chased them with a shot of water. Then he went back into the bedroom, dressed, and checked himself in the mirror as well as the time.

He had five minutes before he had to leave, and he needed to eat when he took his pills. He hurried to his tiny kitchen, pulled open the refrigerator, and grabbed an apple. There was only one but it would have to do for breakfast. He ate it as he left the house and got into his car for the four-mile drive to work.

When he pulled into the lot and parked, there were a lot of people heading the same way he was. They were saying good morning and greeting each other, chatting away. Fisher pushed his hands into his pockets and walked, head slightly down, the way he always did. Into the warehouse, punch in, check the systems, and then out to the yard-control booth near the entrance, where he'd meet incoming drivers and explain where they were to go. That was his day, every day the warehouse was running. He spent a lot of his time either speaking with the drivers or simply sitting and waiting. In his pocket was a small paperback that he could read on his break and lunch.

"Morning," one of the men said as he passed Fisher. Fisher returned the greeting, then sat in his chair and began checking in the first of many trucks waiting to deliver their loads. By the time his morning was over, Fisher had spoken to dozens of drivers coming into the yard and an equal number waiting to be checked out with their loads to be shipped. He was the first and last line of defense in the yard, and Fisher took his job seriously. He was always meticulous and careful, checking each load against manifests and documentation.

"It's lunchtime," Ellen, his supervisor, said as she approached the booth. "I'll take over for you so you can go in and eat." A few months ago, after she realized Fisher was staying in the booth and eating a sandwich at his computer, she had started intervening, spelling him for lunch.

"Thanks."

"You spend way too much time alone," she told him as she settled in the seat. "I did this job for four years before you came, and there were times I wanted to pull my hair out. In summer it was hot as hell, and in winter, cold as blazes."

"I don't mind," Fisher said. "I guess I'm a loner by nature." He turned, waved once, and walked across the yard to the main building and down to the lunchroom.

He stood in line behind the others who were waiting to place their orders. His mind drifted to the night before… and JD. He'd been so nice, and it had felt special to have someone to talk with. He thought about calling him to see if they could get food together again, but all he knew was that JD was a police officer. He didn't know his last name, and it wasn't like it really mattered. JD had been nice to him, but he was really cute…. Okay, JD was hot, smoking hot, so he wouldn't be interested in a skinny guy like him even if JD was gay.

"Can I help you?" the man behind the counter asked, and Fisher realized he'd been staring off into space thinking about JD for a while. Everyone behind him was looking at him and waiting. Fisher swallowed hard and for a second thought about getting out of line and going without lunch.

"A burger, please," he said quietly, "with fries."

"Okay," he said and called in the order, then rang Fisher up before moving on to the next person. Fisher got out of the way and got a cup for water. With his medication he was careful about the amount of caffeine he consumed. It had the effect of intensifying the highs he was trying to manage, just like alcohol intensified the lows, and he didn't need those either. Being on an even keel most of the time was the best he could hope for.

His food arrived, and Fisher sat in his usual place near the wall and pulled the paperback action novel from his pocket. He opened to the place he had stopped and began to read, absently popping fries in his mouth as he turned each page. It wasn't long before he was in the middle of the action, with the bad guys chasing the good guys through the mountains. His heart raced and he continued turning the pages. He picked up his burger with one hand, while still holding the book in the other, and he ate and read, escaping into the world of the author's imagination. It was so much better than his own life and anything he could dream up in his head.

Fisher had lots of stories to tell, but when he tried to write them down, they always came out as a disorganized, jumbled mess and he never got anything finished. In his mind he could tell the story, but between his head, his hands, and then the page, everything got messed up and didn't make sense. Not that it really mattered. No one was going to read them anyway.

He checked the clock and noted that he had ten minutes to finish eating and get back. He ate the last of his lunch and took care of the dishes. Then he put his book in his coat pocket once again and began the walk back out to the yard.

"How was it?" he asked Ellen when he entered the booth and checked the system for status.

"Quiet. You know, with most truckers at lunch too. Did you have a good lunch?"

Fisher shrugged and saw a truck pulling into the yard. Ellen got off the stool and stood nearby while Fisher checked in the truck and waited for the system to figure out where to deliver. Then he directed the driver and gave him his door number. He was just finishing up when the phone rang.

Ellen answered it. She wasn't happy. "All right. We'll make an adjustment in the system. But remind him to follow instructions next time." She hung up. "The truck that we sent to door eighteen went to twenty. Says he didn't like the look of the loading dock. They're going to have it looked at, but we need to switch it in the system and put eighteen as unavailable."

Fisher got to work making the change. It wasn't as easy as it sounded. The old entry had to be backed out and then the new entry entered. Once that was done, the system would need to recalculate and that would take additional time, especially with all the other system processing going on. "It's all set," he told her a few minutes later. "They should be good to go."

Ellen made the call and then reached for the door. "You need to get out more, Fisher. I worry about you."

"I'm fine."

She paused, and Fisher turned away from his computer screen. "You may think so, but I've known you for a while. You were always quiet, but not this quiet. You've pulled away from everyone and into yourself. We used to eat lunch together, and we talked. Then you started staying out here…."

Fisher sighed. "I'll try."

"Good," Ellen said and left the booth.

Fisher knew he'd given an empty promise. The only reason he and Ellen had eaten lunch every day before she got her well-deserved promotion was because she came to his desk at noon each day to get him for lunch. Otherwise he'd have sat alone and read, like he did now.

The flow of trucks slowed in the afternoon, since most deliveries were scheduled in the morning, but outgoing trucks picked up, so he had to check them out and verify seals and manifests. By the time second shift came on at five, he was tired and ready to go home. Fisher closed down the booth and logged out of the system before getting all his things and locking up. Then he walked back to the office to punch out and joined the flow of people heading home.

Sometimes he felt like one of those drones that they flew over Afghanistan. He'd heard talk on the news about them, and he figured he was the human version. Oh, he had a mind, but most of the time he felt like someone else was in control and he was just going through the motions of what he was supposed to do. It hadn't always been like that. Things had been wild years ago, before he'd been placed on his medication. He'd gone to parties, drinking and having fun. He knew that because people told him. He didn't really remember most of it. Parts of his memories were a blur and had been for a while.

Fisher got in his car and pulled out of the lot, heading home to his apartment. Unlike some of the guys at the warehouse, he only had a short drive. One man he'd heard talking in the cafeteria drove almost an hour to get to work. That was something Fisher couldn't comprehend, but he kept it to himself. He liked his short drive down the rural road, approaching the buildup of town and then pulling into his familiar, comfortable piece of the world.

Once he'd parked, Fisher remembered that he didn't have anything in the house to eat, so he backed the car out and drove over to the grocery store to do his weekly shopping. He wasn't one of those guys with a shopping list, but he didn't wander up and down the aisles either, trolling for whatever caught his eye. He mostly bought the same things and knew where they were, what they cost, and how much he needed. The checkout girl could almost tell him the amount he was going to spend before she rang up his things. Like many things in his life, it rarely varied and he didn't make any effort to change it.

By the time he got back home, he was even more tired. He unloaded the car and went inside, unpacked the groceries, put them away, and hung up his coat. It wasn't bad outside. The sky was clear. It was going to be cold, judging by the cloudless blue sky, and since he wasn't hungry yet, he pulled his coat back on and decided to go for a walk.

As soon as he stepped outside, he plunged his hands into his pockets, tightened his coat around him, and headed for the square at a brisk pace. Movement helped keep him warm, but he had no place to go, so he ended up in his usual place on the square, sitting on the bench that sat right in front of the veterans' memorial. He thought it was perfect. The memorial provided a windbreak, and there was a space between the trees, so sometimes the sun would shine on him. There were a lot of people in the square, familiar faces. Not that he talked to any of them, nor they to him. There was the woman who sat on the bench on the corner across the street in front of the church. He knew her. She always sat there, watching people pass, smiling at the small children, sometimes saying a word or two before returning to her rigid posture. Fisher called her Grandma because she acted like the town grandmother. And there was the kid who sat on the bench right next to the courthouse. He had a wild look in his eyes, and Fisher had often wondered if something was wrong with him. Sometimes the kid rocked back and forth slightly, never saying a word.

Of course there were the scooter people—mostly old retirees with nothing to do who rode their motorized wheelchairs around like they were regal chariots. When they approached, you got out of the way because they thought they owned the sidewalk. Other than a few people, no one really talked to each other. Some of the scooter people were friends, and they met up to talk or ride for coffee, but everyone else existed in their own little world, one visible to the entire town, but never really noticed by anyone. They were there, sitting, the forgotten people. Fisher used to feel sorry for them when he'd pass the square, and now he was one of them, sitting on his bench, coat pulled tight with nothing to do.

"Hey, man," a young man whispered as he approached. "You got a cigarette?"

"No," Fisher answered. "Sorry."

"No problem." He smiled, showing a gap where a front tooth had once been. The dark-skinned man looked nice enough, but Fisher was wary. Being approached here wasn't normal. "You need some help? Something to make you happy and forget?"

Fisher had figured. "No, thanks." He smiled slightly, pressing harder to the bench like it was going to protect him if the man got nasty.

"It's cool," he said and sauntered off, long coat billowing in the breeze. Fisher watched him go for a second and then looked away. It wasn't good to get too close a look at a guy like that.

A police cruiser glided down the street toward the square, and Fisher wondered if JD was in it. He couldn't see inside, but his heart did a little flutter, and he smiled slightly at the idea. He thought about waving, just to see, but the cruiser made a turn and continued on. Maybe he should have pointed out where the drug-dealing dude had gone. Not that he had any proof, and it probably wasn't a good idea to start trouble. It had a way of finding him on its own without his asking for it.

Fisher knew it was probably best if he walked back home. It was only going to get colder, but he wanted to sit a little while longer. He knew he was being dumb, but this was the place where he'd met JD, and he was hoping JD might want to talk again or something. He didn't have his number. He knew he was a police officer, but that was all. They'd met here in the square, so he wanted to see if JD would walk by again.

Another police car passed the square. This one slowed, made the turn at the square, and then the turn behind the square toward the Gingerbread Man bar. Fisher followed it with his eyes, and when the car pulled to a stop, he waited to see if the officer got out. Of course, when he did it wasn't JD, but Fisher did recognize Red. He figured this was his chance. So he got up and wandered over.

"Fisher?" Red asked as he approached.

"Hi, Red." He flashed a smile.

"We got a report of someone soliciting. Have you seen anything?" Red asked.

"A guy came through, black kid, asked if I wanted something to make me happy. When I said I didn't, he moved on." Fisher spoke softly. "He was missing a front tooth but looked all right otherwise." Fisher took a step back at Red's stormy look. "I don't do none of that anymore," spilled out of his mouth before he could stop it. "Not that I did a lot, but I was pretty messed up. I told him no, and he walked over toward the side street beside the church."

"He isn't going to find any business there," Red said, then made a call in a police code of some sort. Just as he did, the guy raced out of the alley, tails of his coat flying, with JD on his heels. JD ran like the wind, strides long and fluid. Fisher couldn't take his eyes off him even as Red got back in the car and drove away, sirens blaring. The noise bounced off the facades of the buildings, echoing from all directions and overlapping until it felt like a drill in Fisher's head, but he didn't look away until JD tackled the man to the ground. That was the last he saw because Red's car pulled up, blocking the view.

Fisher waited and watched the activity in the surrounding area, wondering if he could go over under the guise of seeing what was going on and maybe catch JD's eye, but he was working, and Fisher wasn't really interested in the drug dealer seeing him speaking with the police. No use asking for trouble. So he went back to his bench and sat down, the cold instantly seeping through his clothes. Maybe it would be best if he went home, he thought again. He could be alone in his own apartment just as well as he could here, and it was warmer too.

But Fisher stayed where he was anyway and watched the officers as they loaded the man into the back of the police car, which Red drove away. Fisher expected JD to go as well, but he saw him still standing on the sidewalk. JD looked from side to side, then crossed the street at a jog.

"Hi, Fisher," JD said as he approached.

"Officer," Fisher said formally, wondering what kind of stop this was. He liked JD; he was a nice guy. But he still wasn't sure what the deal was, and he'd already learned the hard way that hope could be a dangerous thing.

"What are you doing out here?" JD asked gently. "It's too cold to be sitting on a bench. You'll get sick, and then where will you be?"

"I needed to get out of the house." It sounded lame even to his ears, but he wasn't going to say he'd been sitting out there hoping to see JD. "I saw you running after that guy. You're fast." JD began walking toward the street, and as if JD had a string tied to him, Fisher followed right along. "Isn't it too cold for you to be out too? Don't they give you a car or something?"

"Yeah, they do, but I had to catch the suspect, and Red said you could identify him. Said he tried to sell to you."

Fisher shook his head. "He approached me, but in that way they have that can be denied. Nothing solid, just the usual wink and nudge."

JD nodded. "He had stuff on him, so we got him for possession."

"There's been a lot of activity recently," Fisher said. He sat on his bench often enough and knew what to look for, so he saw plenty of guys approaching folks, leading them away to make deals, stuff like that. "How late do you work?"

"Late," JD said, and Fisher nodded, lowering his gaze as they headed along the sidewalk. It took him about two minutes to realize that JD was walking him home.

"You know, I'll be okay on my own. I'm not anyone that these guys are going to bother with." He shoved his hands deep into his pockets and positioned them against his body for warmth.

"Why do you say it like that?" JD asked.

Fisher stopped and shrugged. "It's just the way it is. I'm one of those guys who sits on a bench in the square because he has nothing better to do. People walk by all day. We watch them sometimes, but they don't see us. Not really. We're like part of the bench itself. It's like that to the druggies too. I'm surprised that guy you took down stopped by me today. I've seen him before, with his expensive leather coat and gap-toothed grin. He strides through the square like he owns it and never sees anyone. I'm sure you've done it too." Fisher hazarded a glance at JD. "Not that you've done anything wrong. It's not like I'm the most memorable person."

"I saw you yesterday, twice. So I don't think I fall into that category." JD sounded miffed.

"Okay." He didn't want to argue, but Fisher knew he was right. He was forgettable and easy to write off and put away. *Don't look at Fisher and he'll just go away.* And that's what had happened with his family and the people who had once been in his life. They'd stopped looking, and he'd in effect gone away.

"We're going out after our shift again. Would you like to come along?"

"To Applebee's?" Fisher asked.

"Yeah. We could go to the Gingerbread Man, but Terry says the menu is better at Applebee's, and there are only so many places that stay open that late in town. Most close before our shift ends. I could pick you up at your apartment building after my shift, if you like."

Fisher nodded before he could think. He wanted to ask JD why he was doing this, but he didn't because he was afraid of the answer. He knew he was a pretty pathetic person, spending a lot of his time sitting on the square, and JD probably felt sorry for him. The thing was, he didn't want to hear the words. Then, for an hour or so, he could hope that JD and his friends liked him as opposed to only tolerating his company.

"I need to get back to my vehicle and on patrol, but you go get warm, and I'll see you a little after eleven." JD turned away and started back toward the corner before stopping. "Can I get your number so I can text you in case I'm going to be late?"

Fisher told him the number, and JD pulled out his phone. Fisher's cell phone rang a few seconds later and then silenced. JD held up his hand and strode back toward the corner, leaving Fisher wondering what was going on, but in a good way.

As soon as JD was out of sight, he went inside and up to the second floor, let himself into his apartment, and started some dinner. He ate and spent the evening in front of the television, watching the clock a little too closely. Then, when eleven o'clock rolled around, he held his phone on his lap waiting for it to buzz and tell him that JD had to work late or that he wasn't coming at all. Instead, a few minutes later it chimed with a text that read, *5 min*, and a smiley face.

Fisher's heart went into overdrive, and he hurried to the bathroom to make sure he wasn't too big a mess. He checked that he'd taken his evening pills and washed his face and hands, then gave his hair a comb. Then he hurried out and grabbed his coat and gloves.

He left his apartment and reached the bottom of the stairs, seeing JD peering through the window. He opened the door and stepped out. "Are Terry and Red coming?"

"Yes. So are Carter and Donald. I work with Carter, and Donald is a social worker," JD said as he pulled open the car door. Fisher had never had anyone hold a door for him. He raised his eyebrows but got in and waited while JD hurried to the driver's side. "I understand they have a son, and that he's staying with a friend for a few days. They rarely go out because of Alex, but they're taking advantage of some kid-free time." JD started the engine and pulled out.

"Are all your friends gay couples?" Fisher asked, hoping for a little clarity.

"Pretty much, so far. Like gathers to like sometimes, and Carter and Red have been really friendly and tried to include me in things." JD took the back way through town toward the restaurant.

"I guess the like-to-like thing is true. I don't know if there are any gay couples or parts of couples where I work."

JD reached across and gripped his knee for a second. "It's okay. You're meeting some people now." JD withdrew his hand, and Fisher assessed the unexpected touch. Heat had instantly flared through him before Fisher could think about it, and by the time he got his mind around the sensation, it was already gone. "Carter has been on the force for a few years, and his specialty is computers and data. He can root out information from places no one else can."

Fisher swallowed and wondered what Carter would find out about him if he looked.

They reached the restaurant and got out. It was bone-chillingly cold, but at least it wasn't snowing. That was an improvement. Fisher did notice that by the time they reached the door of the restaurant, JD was shivering. "You need to get a better coat and some heavy gloves and maybe a hat. If this is cold for you, it's going to get worse."

"That's what they tell me. I went to the sporting goods store to see what they had, but it wasn't helpful, and the department stores have these things that cost an arm and a leg."

Fisher looked to the side and pointed. "Go right over there. The TJ Maxx has a bunch of coats and things—good heavy ones at really great prices. That's where I get most of my clothes." He didn't add that it was all he could afford. "They should be open in the morning, so you could go before work."

"Cool," JD said, and they went inside.

Fisher recognized Red and Terry. They were at a larger table, and they all stood as he and JD approached. JD made introductions, and they sat down and were given menus. At least tonight Fisher wasn't out of it the way he'd been the night before. He felt good, and when the others all ordered beers, he thought about it, but got a Sprite instead.

"How did you and JD meet?" Carter asked, and Fisher wasn't sure how to answer.

"JD brought Fisher last night, and we had a good evening. He works over at one of the warehouses out by I-81," Terry answered. "You seemed a little under the weather, but you're looking better now," he said to Fisher. The server passed out their drinks, and Terry sipped his. "Did everything go okay today?"

"It was another day. My job isn't that exciting," Fisher said and turned to Carter and Donald. "JD said you have a little boy?"

"Yeah. We adopted him a little while ago. He's something else. He's having a sleepover with his friend Isaac at Kip and Jos's. Those two are almost inseparable."

"They've both had a hard time of it," Donald said. "It isn't that surprising that they'd bond." He leaned closer to Carter. Even if Fisher hadn't known they were together, their need to be close would have been a dead giveaway. "I'm just happy that Alex is acting like a normal kid after what he went through."

Fisher turned to JD for an explanation, but JD looked at Carter and Donald. "Alex was abused before we found him," Carter said very seriously. "Now it's like he's a completely different child: outgoing, energetic, running and yelling all the time. But that's enough about children. Donald and I will talk about Alex for hours if you let us."

"Hey," Red interrupted. "I was going to ask you. I found some old things of mine, and I was wondering if you wanted them for Alex. They're airplane models. I made them when I was a teenager, and I was going through some old boxes and found them. They're colorful."

"Alex loves planes, so that would be awesome."

"I used to do those models too," Fisher said. "Remember all the tiny nobs and detailed painting on the instrument panels that no one was ever going to see unless you looked just right through the clouded glass windows?" He smiled. "A few years ago I bought one and decided to try doing some again. It was fun. I finished one and then wondered what to do with it."

"That was always the problem. Once you were done, the fun was over," Red said. "I even found a few kits that were still in the packages. I was going to throw them in a yard sale…." His gaze met Fisher's. "If you'd like them, you're more than welcome to them. I don't have much time now."

"Yeah," Fisher said. "That would be fun." He had nothing but time, so something to occupy it would be good. He also needed things to concentrate on, and inconsequential activities that required concentration were good therapy. "Would you excuse me?" he asked and pushed his chair back so he could go to the restroom before they ordered.

He hurried to the back and did his business, then washed his hands and left the bathroom to return to the table.

"On a bench at the square?" he heard one of the guys ask. Fisher couldn't discern which one. He stopped still, knowing that tone all too well.

"Yeah. I saw him and my gaydar pinged so loud in my ears I thought I'd go deaf. He was really cute and alone, so I went to talk to him."

Fisher didn't want to seem like he was spying, so he continued to the table and took his seat, trying not to turn and smile at JD after what he'd heard. JD thought he was really cute. Well, cute wasn't exactly the word he'd hoped would describe him, but he'd take it. At least he knew that JD helping him hadn't only been a cop thing. "What did I miss?"

"JD was telling us how you met," Terry said. "Granted, Red and I knew some of it already. Carter was less than politically correct, and we were just reminding him that he's not the smoothest cream in the dairy case."

Fisher had to laugh; there was no way to stop it. "You'll say just about anything, won't you?"

"It's the beer," Red said. "Give him one and he's talkative, two and he's dancing on the table, three and he passes out under it." He asked their server for water when she passed by, and she said she'd be right back.

This was so nice. Thankfully, after that the conversation shifted to Terry and his big mouth. Of course with three police officers at the table, after that the conversation turned to work.

"This coke is some nasty stuff," Kip said.

31

"Yeah," Red agreed. "We took down a big source of drugs a while ago, and things calmed down a lot." Terry moved closer to Red, and Fisher knew there was a story there somewhere. "But it was only a matter of time before someone moved in to fill the void."

"I'm surprised it took this long," Carter chimed in.

"What's happened the past few days is just the tip of the iceberg," JD cautioned. "Things are going to get worse. Someone is pushing this stuff pretty hard, and it's fast becoming the dose of choice." He slid his arm around Fisher's shoulder. "You were a big help today."

"Not really."

"Yeah, you confirmed the description of the guy we caught."

"I won't have to testify or anything, will I?" Fisher asked, his stomach turning in knots. He tried to keep his voice level and ask the question as though it was only idle curiosity—rather than something that scared him half to death.

"No. You only helped confirm that we had the right guy," JD said as the server returned with their water and took their orders before hurrying away. The place had pretty much emptied out, and they were most likely the last orders of the evening.

Fisher spent most of the time while they waited for their food listening as the others told stories. He was surprised at some of their choices. Most people told stories of things that made them look good, but these guys told foible stories—about themselves—and then shared the laugh with the others. They were open and honest, without pretense. Laughter came easily, and Fisher wished more than anything that he could feel that ease himself. When the plates arrived, the conversation lulled, but only for a few seconds, and then laughter bubbled up once again.

"That's enough beer," Red scolded Terry. "You are not going to tell the Hershey Park story again."

"Come on, Fisher hasn't heard it," Terry said with a huge grin. "So we're at the park last summer, and they have these huge water slides. Well, we wait in line, and it's Red's turn. He went down, and I heard him whooping through the tube. After two seconds the whoop raises a full octave, and at the bottom I saw Red floundering in the water. After a second his suit follows him out of the slide. He turned to get it and flashed his gorgeous backside for all of Hershey Park to see."

"Not all of us wear those Speedos," Red grumbled.

"Yeah, but it worked out that time, didn't it?" Terry giggled. "I felt so bad because I'd just bought him the suit, and he didn't tell me how loose it was. He wanted to wear it to make me happy, and the slide just whisked it away when it turned him all around." Terry faced Red. "It could have happened to anybody, and half the ladies waiting for their kids got the thrill of a lifetime."

"I think if that happened to me, I'd never be able to show my face again," Fisher said.

"Well...." Terry giggled harder. "Red was showing off one of his better ass... ets." The others laughed, and Red moved Terry's beer away from him while smiling indulgently.

"You were showing off your own assets that day too," Red whispered and then leaned in close for a slight nuzzle. Being around others was really nice, but these couples were so happy that it made Fisher yearn for something he didn't think he could ever have, not with his list of issues. If he tried to catalog them, it would take until the end of time.

"What kind of stories do you have?" Terry asked. He seemed like the table's social director.

Fisher saw everyone look at him. "None like that. I'm not a very exciting person," he demurred and returned his attention to his food, hoping like hell that everyone would move on. They didn't seem to, so Fisher paused, putting down his knife and fork. "About four years ago...." He hated telling this story. "Okay, I was driving this really old car and... I probably shouldn't be telling any of you this."

"Had you been drinking?" Carter asked.

"No. But I was anxious and worried about things. I know I shouldn't drive when I feel distracted."

"You mean like yesterday?" JD asked in a way that wrapped around him.

Fisher nodded. "I don't drive a lot if I can help it. Usually just to work and back, or to the store. But mostly I walk. The thing is, I was nerved up and...." He was rambling and stopped to get his thoughts together. "Sorry," he said and reached for his glass of water, then drank it all in order to combat the heat his nerves were generating. "I pulled to a stop at the light out by the turnpike. I hate that place. It's just before where the lanes branch off and everyone realizes they're in the wrong lane. Well, this guy behind me was paying more attention to where he wanted to be and less to where he was going, and his dump truck smashed into the back of my car. That's all I remember. I came to in the hospital, and they told me I had a concussion."

Donald reached across the table, and Fisher jumped when he touched his hand. "Traumatic brain injury?" he asked.

Fisher nodded. "I lost parts of my memory. So there are lots of things that don't make sense to me." He stopped and lifted his knife and fork.

"It's okay," JD said and patted his leg.

"I wish it was," Fisher said, plowing on. "When I was eight I got this pair of inline skates. I know I did because I've seen pictures, but I don't remember it. My mom told me I'd been asking for them for months and that she went out special to get them, but all I remember is that they were green and I hated the color. So that's what sticks with me—that my mom got me ugly skates. I know it doesn't make sense to you, but the context is gone. So the things most of us have to hold on to, those happy memories, are erased or jumbled." He turned to JD. "You told us about taking your sister hunting. I don't have memories like that. Mine seem normal and like they're real and full, but I know there are parts missing because I've seen proof." He scratched his head, hoping he was making sense.

"What does your family think?" JD asked.

Fisher shrugged. It didn't matter any longer. They'd made their feelings plain on the subject. "They think…." He paused again, every eye at the table on him.

"Hey, it's okay. You don't have to talk about this," JD said.

Fisher nodded and turned back to his wings, using the knife and fork to get at the meat. He didn't look up from his task. It was much better to try to act normal than to see the pity or that confused look most people got when he tried to explain how his head worked.

"What happened to the truck driver?" Carter asked.

"He got cited and stuff, but the company he works for has been stalling all this time." He shrugged once again. There was only so much he could worry about or he'd go into one of his spirals. He'd had enough of them to know when they were coming and what the triggers were.

"But you're doing okay now?" Terry asked.

"Most of the time. My memories aren't coming back, and the doctors said that some things had changed inside that would never be the way they were." That was the way it was, and he'd done the best he could to come to grips with it. "I was out of control for a while because I didn't understand what was happening to me, and I did things I'm not proud of. Some of them I can't remember." And he'd hurt the people in his life in ways he couldn't remember either, but the end result was the same.

"Hey. It's all right," JD said again, and Fisher wished he'd stop saying that. Everyone told him that all the time.

"No, it's not," he said too loudly, pushing JD's hand away and upsetting JD's water glass. Everyone jumped and began tossing napkins on the table to sop it up. Fisher stood and stepped back, trying to clean up another of his messes. "Things will never be all right for me."

"We got it," Donald said levelly as the server came over, helping to clear up the spilled water.

"It's okay, sir. This happens all the time." She grabbed what was left of Fisher's plate of wings—which were now floating in water—and wiped the table. "I'll have the kitchen remake these for you." She hurried away.

Fisher slowly sat back down, wanting to disappear into the floor. "I'm sorry." What the hell else could he say? He was a sorry excuse for a person, and all these people had to be wondering why JD had brought him along. He was better off staying at home… alone.

"It was only some water, and I understand," Donald said.

"You do?" He couldn't help the hint of sarcasm.

"Sure. I bet everyone told you it was all right for a long time as a way to try to keep you quiet and calm. Something would happen, and the people around you were afraid you'd get upset, so they'd tell you it was all right, calm down, and then they'd sweep in and try to make things the way they were."

"And clean up my messes," Fisher added.

"This was an accident. It happens." The look was so firm in Donald's eyes that even though Fisher wanted to argue, it died on his lips. Donald leaned to the side, and his lips curled into a wicked grin.

"Oh no," Carter whispered softly.

Fisher didn't have time to wonder what was going on before Donald had his phone out and was showing him pictures of the most adorable little boy.

"This is Alex. He's five now."

"You don't have to show pictures to everyone we meet," Carter said indulgently.

Donald just ignored him. "He wanted to be a turtle for Halloween, and not one of those ninja kind, but a real turtle, whatever that means. I swore he was going to make me look for a costume until I found one made out of real turtle shell." The phone was passed from person to person.

"He's really adorable," Fisher said.

"I ended up making it for him. Took me three days, eight pokes, a trip to the doctor for a tetanus shot, and I nearly sewed three of my fingers together, but I did it."

"It wasn't that bad," Carter said, rolling his eyes. "Don't be such a drama queen."

"I did have to go to the doctor," Donald said, and Fisher found himself smiling at their antics. The server brought him a fresh plate of wings, and the incident with the water glass seemed forgotten as mirth returned to the table. When Fisher chanced a glance at JD, he was surprised at the warmth in his eyes. Fisher turned away to eat and to try to remember the last time anyone had looked at him that way. The truth was he couldn't remember it at all. Either the memories were gone or they'd never existed. He did know for sure that in the past few years there had been nothing, because that part of his life was largely intact.

"You know, we're going to have to stop making a habit out of closing this place down," Terry said once there was nothing left on the table but dirty dishes and empty glasses. The server had brought their checks, and they were waiting for change. "Maybe next time we can go to the house or something."

"Yeah," Donald said. "But then you'd have to clean up, and this way we pay the bill and someone else does the dishes."

"True," Terry said and stood up, putting on his coat. "We need to get these hard-working law enforcement officers home after their long day of keeping the streets safe."

"You're a pain sometimes," Red scolded.

"It's part of my charm," Terry quipped, and Red hugged him and didn't say anything more. He didn't have to. Fisher turned away for a second, trying not to look. They were in public, but something about the way they looked at each other made Fisher feel like a voyeur, like he was seeing something intimate between them.

"We should go. I know you need to be at work earlier than the rest of us," JD said, and after they said good night to everyone and Fisher was hugged within an inch of his life multiple times, he and JD walked to the door. Fisher paused to put on his coat and gloves, and then they walked out into the clear, cold night to JD's car.

The ride back to Pomfret Street was fast, no more than a few minutes, and too soon they were outside Fisher's building. He got out and was about to say good night when JD hurried around the car to meet him at the front door. "I'm glad you came. It was a nice evening, and they all liked you."

"What's there to like?" Fisher asked and instantly knew he should have kept quiet. On an intellectual level he was aware that insecurity wasn't pretty.

"Plenty. It took guts to tell us what happened and how it affected you." JD was so close, almost too close. Fisher could feel the heat between them battling with the cold in the air, and to his amazement, the warmth was winning… at least for the moment. "Stop being so hard on yourself and worrying about what everybody thinks, and just let Fisher come through."

"How boring would that be?" He expected JD to give him some nice social platitude. But instead, JD leaned closer and then closed the distance between them. Fisher nearly gasped. He was being kissed, like, *really* kissed. JD slowly encircled him in his arms, and his warmth mixed with his own, and then Fisher was flying a little. Thankfully, he remembered to kiss him back, because this was amazing and it would have been a shame to let this go and…. Fisher silenced the rambling commentary in his mind at about the time that JD pulled away.

"Was that boring?" JD asked, and Fisher shook his head, licking his lips to get a last taste of JD from where they still tingled. "I have this theory that it takes two exciting people to make a really exciting kiss, and so far when it comes to kisses, I'm never wrong. So I'd say that was exciting, and therefore we must both be really not boring in order for that to happen. Okay?"

Fisher nodded, because who could argue with logic like that? Hell, who would want to?

"Good." JD leaned in for another kiss, and this time the commentary was silent. Fisher let the kiss and the heat wash over him. By the time JD pulled away this time, Fisher was breathless and a little light-headed.

"I have coffee," Fisher said.

He could see JD considering it when his phone rang. JD answered it and listened. "All right" was all he said before hanging up. "I have to go. Another time for the coffee." JD hurried around the car, and with a final wave, he got in and took off. Fisher went inside and closed the door, still thinking of those kisses and wondering why JD had to rush off.

CHAPTER
Three

JD LIMPED into his apartment three hours after leaving Fisher at his building and fell into bed. A fire had broken out at one of the warehouses outside of town, and the place had gone up quickly. The company handled various cleaning chemicals, and the heat had mixed some of them, creating a combustible situation. Homes downwind had to be evacuated and the entire area sealed off. What a mess. At least the warehouse officials had kept proper records and were able to explain what all of the chemicals were. When JD was sent home, the fire was still burning out of control, but there were only so many hours he could work, and he was supposed to be back on shift in less than eight hours.

He managed to get his shirt, shoes, and socks off before falling on the mattress, punching his pillow a few times, and closing his eyes. That was it. He was out, and the next thing JD knew was his phone ringing again five hours later.

"Hello," he said raspily.

"This is your mother. I hope I'm not waking you," she said as though seven in the morning was too late for any decent person to sleep. "Your aunt's funeral is Thursday. I trust you'll do the right thing and let the family grieve without any unnecessary drama and hubbub."

"Fine. Just e-mail me the details, and I'll be the good son and do what you want." He was too tired to fight her.

"You stopped being the good son when you decided to embarrass your family. I'm just pleased you decided to do the right thing. I'll send you the details."

"Okay," JD said. He waited to see if she would say anything more, but the line remained quiet and eventually dropped. He tossed his phone onto the bed and rolled over, burying his face in his pillow. He was not going to cry over this again. He'd done it once and it was over. Done. There was nothing he could do to change what had happened or to alter his family's feelings about it. They felt the way they felt, and Lord knew his mother would keep things stirred up for everyone if they didn't go along.

He rolled over, facing upward, and closed his eyes, imagining the ceiling was gone and he was outside in a meadow back home, the one his aunt used to take him to for picnics in the summer. The stream nearby ran over the rocks, gurgling and laughing. Aunt Lillibeth was one of a kind. When he and his mother fought, which was regularly, she'd always been there to help pick up the pieces. It was hot in the summer, and he'd play in the cool water while she sat on the bank, watching and laughing along with him. He was going to miss her lightheartedness and ability to laugh and not take things too seriously—a severe contrast to his mother and even his father, her brother. Of course, he couldn't stay in his imagination forever, and he fell back to sleep thinking of her.

When he woke again, he checked the time and got dressed. Then he called the station. They asked him to report for duty right away. The fire was still burning and could be for hours yet.

"We need help patrolling the evacuation zone. Residents have tried to go back in. Also, there are many people trying to get to work at other facilities in the area. It's a plain mess," the fire captain said.

"Okay. I'm on my way. Should I report right out there?"

"Yes. See Cloud. He's handling the assignments for the time being, while the big boys are getting their beauty sleep."

"Thanks," he said. He finished getting ready for the cold before leaving the house and heading out.

As he approached the area, two things quickly became apparent: the roads were clogged with cars, and people were trying to get to work. Officers were attempting to get them turned around, but it was difficult. Word obviously hadn't gotten out as efficiently as it should have, and that meant a lot of inconvenienced people. JD checked in and went to work trying to help control traffic.

"Sir," JD said as he approached the next car and waited for the driver to roll down his window. "The area is closed. You need to turn around and go back the way you came. Turn right to get on I-81."

"But I work over there," he said, pointing to the warehouse a few hundred yards away.

"There may be hazardous chemicals. They've closed for today. All the businesses in this area are evacuated. Please go back." He repeated the same conversation dozens of times as they slowly got traffic moving away from the evacuation zone. As he approached one of the last cars, JD saw a familiar, worried face looking back at him.

"JD, what's going on?" Fisher asked breathlessly. "Someone said one of the warehouses was burning."

"Didn't you watch the news?" JD asked.

Fisher shook his head. "I overslept because of the fun last night, and I hurried here so I wouldn't be late. I usually get to work earlier, but we were scheduled to work late tonight, so they asked me to come in at nine. It isn't Optima, is it?"

Damn, JD wanted to lie and say it wasn't, but he nodded. He saw Fisher's eyes lower, and then he started to shake.

"Oh God."

"It'll be all right." It was the first thing that came out of his lips, and he knew it was the wrong thing to say. "You should go on home and call in to the company headquarters. Let them know you're okay, and they'll tell you what to do, I'm sure."

Fisher nodded. JD could see the pain in his expression. "Okay. I'll go home."

"Call me later if you like. If you want to talk," JD offered and stepped back to allow Fisher to turn around. He wasn't sure if he would, and JD was a little worried about his new friend.

"Is Optima where Fisher works?" Carter asked as he pulled up. "I saw you talking to him."

"Yeah." JD turned, watching where Fisher had gone. "He isn't sure what to do."

"There are going to be a lot of people out of work unless they can find a new location and get it up and running. There isn't going to be anything left of the current location."

"At least the fire is dying, and they're making good progress. I spoke to the fire marshal, and he's hopeful that people will be able to return to their homes in a few hours. This is going to be very messy for a lot of people."

JD nodded. "I'm worried about one person in particular at the moment."

Carter rolled his eyes. "I'll give you that the guy is cute, but what do you see in him?"

JD had to think about his answer. "Do you remember as a kid on Christmas morning, when you came down and first looked at the tree with all the packages, bows, and ribbons? At that moment, anything was possible. There could have been anything in those boxes. Well, a lot of people are like the opened packages. You know who they are and what you're going to get within ten minutes of meeting them. Sometimes you get a real surprise, but mostly they fit a mold and that's all there is to it."

"God, that's a dreary sentiment."

"Yeah. Maybe, and the surprises are usually bad. But Fisher is a wrapped package that no one has bothered to look at. Still waters run deep, and I think there's a lot of depth there." He didn't say that he'd seen some of Fisher's pain in his eyes and it mirrored his own. Fisher had amazing blue eyes, but they were clouded with layers of hurt and longing for what he couldn't have. "I need to get back to work. I'm hoping once I've put in my hours that I can go." He was still tired and could use the chance to get some more rest.

"You have an interesting way of looking at things," Carter said. "Is that a Southern thing?"

"No. I think it's a Burnside thing," he answered flatly and patted the roof of Carter's patrol car. Carter rolled up the window and drove away while JD went back to making sure the evacuation zone remained clear.

HIS SHIFT over, JD had never been so happy to be off work in his life. He stank and felt grubby, but the fire was out and residents had been allowed back into their homes. But his mind would not let go of the devastated look on Fisher's face when he'd heard the news. Throughout the day as he pondered it, he realized he'd witnessed someone who felt their life had come to an end. He kept trying to convince himself that he was imagining things, but deep down he knew he wasn't.

"Call Donald on cell," he instructed the Bluetooth connection in his car as he drove home from the station. The car was just new enough to have the feature and just old enough that it sometimes did the craziest things. There were times when he wanted to strangle his car's voice, but this time it did what he asked.

"JD, what's going on?" Donald answered.

JD heard a crying baby in the background. "Maybe I should ask you that."

"I'm in the office, and they're doing child vaccinations, so all I've heard all day are crying kids. My head is going to explode," he added in a softer tone. "What's up?"

"There was a huge fire today."

"Yeah, I saw it on the news."

"It's where Fisher works," JD said. "I turned him around on the road today and… he looked as though he didn't know what he was going to do."

"Just a second," Donald said, and a few seconds later the background noise was gone. "What do you want from me? I only met him last night for a little while."

"I know," JD said. He probably shouldn't have called. "I don't know what I should do."

"What do you want to do?" Donald asked in his best "psychologist who has you on his couch" voice.

"Thanks." This wasn't helpful.

"I'm serious. I can't crawl into Fisher's head and give you the key to what's going on. I can't do that with Carter, though Lord knows I'd like to sometimes. So what do you want to do?"

"I told him to go home because there was nothing for him there. I want to go see him and make sure he's all right. He seemed so fragile, like he was suddenly made of glass."

"Okay. Let me ask you this: When was the last time you felt that way? Often the answer to questions about others is about putting yourself in their shoes."

JD shivered. He remembered feeling like glass, like he was about to shatter at any moment. Standing in front of his parents, them yelling and then turning their backs on him. All he'd been able to do was stand there, very still, unable to believe or process what was truly happening. Then he'd gone to Aunt Lillibeth and…. JD's head began to throb as he pulled to a stop in front of his house. "I get it."

"Do you know what you're going to do?"

"Yeah. Thanks. I'll talk to you later." He hung up and jammed open the car door. Somehow he managed to make it inside and to the bathroom before he lost what was left of his lunch. When he was done, he rinsed his mouth, staring at himself in the mirror. He was a fraud and he knew it. Always happy on the outside, while hollow and empty on the inside. His job required that he be strong, confident, and sure of himself. When he was out on the street, danger was everywhere, so in addition to bulletproof vests, guns, weapons, and physical fitness, he wrapped himself in an air of confidence and invincibility. It was an image he projected because weakness could be exploited. But that was all an act. He was drawn to Fisher because he saw himself in him, only more intense.

In situations like this, when he was stumped, he'd always called his aunt. But now that wasn't possible, and he was even more on his own. JD took a drink of water and then left the bathroom at a clip. He grabbed a sweater and pulled it on, then got his coat and yanked it over his arms before leaving the house in a rush. Instead of driving, he strode down the sidewalk, stretching his legs, hands stuffed in his coat pockets, eyes set firmly ahead. Anyone in his way had better get out of it, because he was on a mission.

JD wasn't sure where he'd check first, but his legs took him to the square and there Fisher was, sitting on the same bench, examining his shoes, arms and head nearly curled in on himself, like he was trying to be as small as possible. JD watched him and wondered if he should say something. Instead, he sat down next to Fisher and waited. Words seemed hollow when you felt like Fisher did. JD didn't fully understand the cause, but he knew the feeling of loss and being shattered. After a few minutes he found himself folding inward too, becoming introspective.

JD didn't feel it at first, but the warmth seeping in told him that Fisher had moved closer. He raised his head, pulling out of thoughts of his aunt and the warmth that had always surrounded her. Fisher's hand was next to his, enshrouded in a leather glove, but JD placed his on top of it anyway and smiled slightly when Fisher's fingers curled around his.

"Sometimes I know I'm being stupid about things, but I don't know how to stop it," Fisher said.

"What did your work say?" JD asked. It was easier to try to help Fisher with his problem than it was to face his own loss and fears.

"That they don't know anything yet. They did say that they would be paying us for a while, and that once they made a decision about the future, they'd let us know."

"All right. So it seems like you have a few days of unexpected vacation. Why don't you enjoy them if you can? Optima is going to need a warehouse, and they're going to have to replace the product they lost, so it stands to reason that they're going to need people they can trust in this new warehouse."

"But what if they decide to move the warehouse to Kansas or Ohio or something? I can't afford to move there." Fisher raised his head. "I can't go looking for a new job, not right now. I don't meet new people well, and when I go into those offices, I freeze up and my mouth works, but nothing comes out and I look like a stupid fish."

JD chuckled, and Fisher smiled a little before continuing. "Since the accident I don't do so well in a lot of situations," Fisher went on. "Rooms full of people overwhelm me. At work I sit in the little house at the edge of the yard to guide the trucks where they need to go. Most of the time I'm alone, and that works for me. There's structure and routine, and I do well with that." Fisher tightened his hold. "I used to be like everyone else. Well, mostly like everyone else, before the accident, and now it's hard to do some of the things everyone else does."

"Do you go to a doctor?" JD asked.

"Yeah, every month. The medication I'm on needs constant adjustment." He looked over, and JD saw his cheeks redden. "People think that you take a few pills and everything is fine, but it's not. I'm never going to be like I was before the accident." Fisher released his hand and slowly got to his feet. "Sitting here isn't going to make anything any easier or change anything."

"Maybe not, but at least it's not too cold," JD said.

Fisher sat back down. "Why were you here?" he asked.

"I came to make sure you were okay."

"But you seemed as low as I get sometimes. What happened?"

JD paused. "My aunt died yesterday. The funeral will be on Thursday, and I think I'm missing her." He turned to face Fisher. "You know that person in the family who gets you? The one you're close to and whatever happens, they're always there, no matter what? That was my aunt. I don't think I'd ever have reached adulthood with a shred of sanity without her. She was my dad's older sister. Never married and always said she never had time for a man, and if she needed one there were plenty she could rent."

Fisher chuckled. "She sounds wonderful."

"She was…. Aunt Lillibeth used to drive up to the house in one of her huge cars, and we'd all pile in and she'd drive us into town with the top down, having the time of our lives. My mother use to scowl about it no end, but Daddy had a soft spot for his sister and would never hear a word against her."

"So why aren't you going to the funeral? I'm sure they'd let you off to go. Most places do have funeral leave."

"I'm not welcome as far as my family is concerned," JD said.

Fisher nodded. "I understand that well." He paused and bit his lower lip. "Do you want to talk about it?"

"God, no," JD answered, and they shared a smile. "I think we've both had enough depressing thoughts for one day." He checked his watch as his stomach grumbled. Now he was hungry. "I was going to try to find something light for dinner. Things got a little woofy earlier, so I need to be careful."

"I have fresh bread and was going to make pasta. You're welcome to join me. I have enough."

JD thought a minute. "I have some root beer at home. It's the really good kind, craft brewed with sugar cane. I could get that."

"Sounds like a plan," Fisher said.

They started walking. At Fisher's building, JD had an urge to kiss him good-bye, but instead he said he'd be back and continued down the block and then over to his house. He went right to the fridge and got the root beer. He tried to think of anything else he should bring, but he left with only that and got into his car. It seemed stupid to drive just a few blocks, but it would be cold later and the walk much more miserable to his Southern bones.

JD was lucky enough to find a parking space near Fisher's building and went inside. He expected to have to be buzzed in and was surprised that the outer door just opened. Once he opened the door, he checked and found the latch broken.

"Go away!" drifted down the stairs from the floor above.

"Why did you send the cops on me?" a gruff voice demanded. JD set the soda down and moved forward, slowly climbing the stairs. A black man stood in a doorway, blocking it open. The last time JD had seen him, he was facedown on the sidewalk after JD had tackled him to the ground for dealing and then trying to flee. His heart pounded with excitement as he pulled out his phone and made a quick call.

"I don't think you want to do that," JD snapped, using his voice as a weapon.

"What's it to you?" he sneered back. "My friend and I were just having a discussion. You should move along." The way he lifted his lips to try to look menacing might have worked on someone else, but it wasn't going to stop JD.

"Actually, since you're out on bail, it's quite a bit to me. I heard you threatening him, and you're not welcome here. The police are already on their way."

"What's all this to you?"

"I'm the guy who caught you yesterday." JD grabbed him by the arm, turned him against the wall, and held his hands behind him. "It isn't your lucky day, now is it? Bail is going to be revoked, and you're going to sit until you're tried, and then it's off to prison." He held the man down until his fellow officers arrived. JD explained what had been happening, and once the guys had talked to Fisher, they took Gap-Tooth away.

"Are you okay?"

"Yeah. He didn't hurt me," Fisher said, but he looked pale.

"Was the door lock broken before?" JD asked.

"No. He must have done it. I'll have to call the landlord and have him fix it. He's not going to be happy."

"It's not your fault," JD said. "I need to go get what I brought. I'll be back." He turned and hurried down the stairs, grabbed the six-pack of warming root beer, and returned. The guy must have followed him and Fisher from the square when they were walking back. JD hadn't noticed anyone, but then he hadn't been watching either. "I should have been paying more attention on our way back."

"You think he followed us?" Fisher asked, and JD nodded. "Yeah, I suppose. I didn't notice him, but how else would he know where to find me?" Fisher closed the door and locked it.

The apartment was small but warm, with furniture that had history. JD handed Fisher the soda, and he took it into the tiny kitchen while JD sat on the sofa in the living room. "I have some cheese and crackers," Fisher said, bringing a plate and then setting it on the coffee table. "I don't get much company."

The apartment was immaculate, without a speck of dust or stray pile of paper. "Are the furnishings family pieces?"

"Yes. A lot of them came from my grandmother. She had a big house out in Old Mooreland, and when she died, we all got to choose what we wanted. I was moving out at that time, so I took a lot of things to set up my first place, and I've had them ever since." Fisher hovered and then hurried away, returning a few minutes later with glasses of ice and bottles of the soda JD had brought. "I know you said that being a policeman ran in your family."

"No. The law runs in my family. My grandfather was a judge and was influential in a number of important cases. He was also able to turn that position into a way to make a great deal of money. I don't know exactly how, because no one talks about it. My father is the senior partner in a large Charleston law firm. He handles big cases and knows everyone important in the government. My parents were less than pleased when I decided to go into law enforcement. They wanted me to follow in my father's footsteps, take over the firm, marry a Southern belle, and have quiet, handsome, respectable children." He took the glass Fisher handed to him.

"Do they know you're gay?" Fisher asked.

"Oh, yeah. But that doesn't matter. I should still do what was expected—marry some woman I don't love to fulfill whatever illusions they have. I couldn't do that, but my cardinal sin was deciding to make up my own mind. I went to the police academy, graduated at the top of my class, and was hired by Charleston for the police force right out of the academy. That's a huge deal. Usually they hire officers with experience from other departments, but they took me right off. Do you think my parents were proud?" JD shook his head. "Nope."

"What about your sister?"

"Rachel is pretty cool when she's alone, but she's never alone anymore, and she needs to toe the line. She went to law school, and Dad is grooming her to take over the firm now."

"And you didn't fit the mold?" Fisher asked as he stood and went into the kitchen. "I know what that feels like." Pots banged more loudly than was necessary and then quieted. "Sorry. I am listening, but I need to get the pasta water boiling." He turned on the tap and filled the pot, then put it on the stove.

"Where was I? Yeah. No, I didn't fit their mold, but I thought they'd come around and accept who I was. Well," he sighed, "the Burnside family proves that denial isn't just a river in Egypt. They live in it each and every day. If something doesn't fit the image, they ignore it, fight it, or if all else fails, cut it out and throw it away." There was more to it than that, but he'd talked plenty, and the evening was becoming one heck of a downer.

"Let's talk about something more pleasant than family disappointment. I'm getting the idea we could fill a book with our experiences."

"Yeah. Let's talk something more pleasant. How about ethnic genocide?"

"Or perhaps the plight of Syrian refugees?" Fisher offered.

JD smiled. He liked that Fisher got his sense of humor. "Okay, so no genocide, refugees, and let's skip politics, and religion for good measure," JD stood up. "That doesn't leave much…." He grinned and moved even closer to Fisher. "Happy subject?" he asked, and Fisher nodded.

"Something maybe even exciting?" JD said, and Fisher's lips parted, his eyes widening, cheeks pinking. "Maybe even tinglingly so."

Fisher's breathing increased as JD gently stroked Fisher's slightly stubbled cheek. Fisher leaned into the touch, and JD couldn't resist.

Last night those full, plump lips had tasted so sweet, and he went in. Sure enough, it was exactly as he remembered, only sweeter and hotter without the chill from the air to cool them off. Damn, when he drew Fisher to him, he came so willingly, shaking as JD held him.

"Have you been kissed before?" JD asked when they came up for air.

"Yes, but before the accident. I dated a few guys." Fisher stiffened.

"Were you dating someone when you had the accident?" JD asked, and Fisher nodded. "Oh gosh." He could see that he'd hit the bull's-eye just from his expression. He needed to learn to keep his mouth shut.

"His name was Gareth. He was Irish and gorgeous with slightly red hair, muscles, and a smile that could light up a room. I used to wonder what he saw in me, but he was attentive, kind, caring, and eye rolling at the right times, if you know what I mean. That I remember, and I also remember his visit to the hospital after I'd woken up. We'd talked about moving in together, but when he brought me home, he took me to my place and said I probably needed some time to rest. The following day he came by to say that things weren't working out and that it would be best if we stopped seeing each other."

"The bastard," JD swore.

"Yeah. I needed help to do everyday things. My hands shook and I could walk, but only slowly. Gareth took one look at me and bolted as fast as he could. Since then there hasn't been anyone. Why would they bother when they could have someone that's whole and not a bundle of problems, mood swings, and bouts of depression? I saw Gareth a year ago. He had this stunning man on his arm, and they were wandering downtown. Window-shopping, by the look of it. Actually, I think they were walking down the street, admiring themselves in the various windows."

JD smiled.

"I hope he's happy," Fisher said.

"To hell with that," JD countered. "I hope he gets crabs, his nuts blow up and explode, and then his dick shrivels to the size of a button mushroom."

Fisher tried to look horrified and then burst out laughing. "Dang, that feels good. I haven't been able to laugh about anything to do with him in a long time." Fisher leaned closer, putting his head on JD's shoulder. "Part of the traumatic brain injury thing is that it's hard to let go. With memories missing, you tend to latch onto what you have, and so forgetting something becomes harder. Good and bad tend to stay around." Fisher didn't move, and JD realized how good it felt to hold someone and be held in return. "I know you've had kisses before."

"How?"

"Because you're a good kisser."

"Yeah. I dated another guy while I was at the academy, but he was so deep in the closet he'll probably never see the light of day again. I dated another officer on the force, but we avoided disaster and decided to be friends. He now lives in Key West with his husband, and if I'm up-to-date, a house full of kids—triplets or something. Apparently the artificial insemination took really well."

Fisher chuckled. "I don't think I want children."

"O… kay."

Fisher straightened up. "I like kids and get along with them really well. But I don't think I should subject a child to the mood swings that I can get sometimes. It's not fair to them not to have a parent who's levelheaded and able to make well-reasoned decisions some of the time. What if I'm in a depression and forget to feed the baby or make dinner because I can't function?" Fisher shook his head. "That's not right."

JD opened his mouth to tell Fisher that everything in his life didn't have to come back to his injury and illness. But who was he to say what the truth was? Fisher had lived it, and JD had only met him a few days ago. How did he know what was right?

"I need to put the pasta in," Fisher said as he moved out of JD's arms. They felt instantly empty and the room cooler without Fisher's furnace-like heat pulsing next to him. Fisher worked quietly and with all his attention on his task. It was only adding pasta to water and then getting the sauce heated, but Fisher was intent on what he was doing. "Do you think the guy who was here will come back?" Fisher lifted his gaze, and it took JD a second to register the complete change of subject.

"I'll check tomorrow and make sure he's going to remain in custody. His bail will be revoked for breaking in, and I can make sure the report states that he followed you and was harassing you. The fact that he was out on bail less than a day and was already a threat means he isn't going to get a second chance. I wouldn't want to be the person who put up that bail."

"Me either," Fisher said and went back to stirring his sauce. "But will I have other people bothering me now? All I did was talk to Red for a few minutes, and I don't think he would have said anything." Fisher's hand shook, and he switched to stirring with the other one.

"I think it was one guy. But you have my number, and you can call me anytime if you don't feel safe. If I'm working or on a call, I have friends who will come." Damn, it was surprising how protective he felt toward Fisher. Yes, it was in his nature, but he didn't get the urge to wrap the general public in a blanket and padding so that nothing could harm them.

Fisher nodded but still seemed really nervous and jittery. Once the pasta was done, he took it off the stove, the pot clanging on the burner. JD grabbed the potholder off the counter and gently helped Fisher drain the pasta. Fisher stood back, shaking, and then actually began pacing the tiny floor of the kitchen. Every time he passed, his hand brushed JD's back.

"Where are the plates?" JD asked, trying to act normally and hoping whatever had gotten hold of Fisher would pass. He wasn't sure what to do. Fisher pointed, and JD got them. He mixed the pasta and sauce and placed it in the bowl. He wasn't sure what else Fisher was planning, but he took the bowl to the small dining table along with the plates.

JD managed to find the cutlery, got two more root beers, and then he guided Fisher to the table.

"I have some bag salad and dressing in the refrigerator," Fisher said. He jumped up and began rummaging around, the energy rolling off him in waves. He returned a few minutes later with a bowl of mixed greens and a bottle of dressing that he set on the table.

It was like eating with a frenetic rabbit. Fisher couldn't sit still, and JD wondered what he could do to calm him down a little.

"Is this one of the wild times?" JD asked.

"I think so." Fisher stopped eating and closed his eyes. "Sometimes I don't know when I'm having them until it's too late."

"I don't think there's anything to be nervous about. I'm here and I'll do all I can to keep you safe."

Fisher nodded and after a few minutes seemed to calm down. He kept his eyes closed, breathing deeply. Eventually Fisher excused himself and left the room. JD heard him in the bathroom, and when he returned he was still as wide-eyed but seemed less agitated. "I have some medication to take when it gets like this. I have to be careful, though."

"It's a battle for you, isn't it?" JD asked.

"Yes. It can be. The thing is, I've become aware that I'm different and what a problem feels like. I only took one pill, and it will start to work pretty soon. I never take more than that unless it's really bad and I'm bouncing off the walls. The bad part is that the active times feel pretty good. I have energy and it seems like I can take on the world. It's the low times that are really hard."

"So what was this?" JD asked. "You don't have to answer if you don't want to."

"An attack of nerves. I get those sometimes too." Fisher sighed. "Can we talk about something—anything—other than this?" He picked up his fork and began to eat again. "Most people around me talk about my illness, like it's the thing to do."

"Your family does that?"

"They used to. We don't see each other anymore." Fisher looked down at his plate and continued eating. Just like at the restaurant, every motion was precise. Somehow Fisher caught only three strands of spaghetti on his fork, twirled it and ate it, then repeated the motion again with the next bite.

JD lowered his gaze and concentrated on his own meal. "Damn," he muttered, and then he hoped Fisher hadn't heard him. No family or friends, from the look of it. In his own mind, JD had thought he'd gotten the short end of the stick with his family, and he'd gone on and on about how they treated him. Fisher had less support than JD, and he hadn't wallowed in it or gone into a litany of his troubles. In fact, he'd only mentioned it because JD had brought it up.

"Tomorrow I have to work really early," JD said. "They're changing my shifts around. The department thinks there are some elements that have been analyzing our schedules so they know when shifts are changing and things like that. I should be off in the late afternoon, and maybe we could wander around the antique stores or something." Given the apartment, JD thought that might be something Fisher would like.

"That isn't necessary," Fisher said. "I know what you're trying to do, and you don't have to. I'm not some lost soul that you need to rescue or some charity case that you spend time with because you think it's your good deed for the week. You're a nice guy, JD, and you could have lots of guys anytime you want. You know that. I'm fine, really, and I don't want to be your pet project."

"Is that what you think this is?" JD asked.

"What the hell else could it be? Face it. You saw me on the square, felt sorry for me, and thought I might need some help, so you got me some food. And you did the same thing last night. Today you realized that the place I work at burned to the ground, so what happened? Your protective cop instincts kicked in, and you decided to try to help." Fisher set his fork and spoon down on his now empty plate. "There's no need for you to spend all your free time with me. You have friends—people who are a hell of a lot more fun than I am to go out with." He lifted his bottle of root beer. "I'm a broken-down person who has to spend his days remembering to take pills so he doesn't flip out and embarrass everyone around him." Fisher upended the bottle, drinking the last of it.

JD sat still, stunned. It took a lot to surprise him, but dang, that was one hell of a speech.

"Finish your dinner and then say good night. It's for the best." The finality in Fisher's voice rang off the walls like a firework shell echoing over an empty field.

JD looked for some sign that Fisher was joking with him or really didn't mean what he'd said, but there was nothing at all but a dead serious expression. Fisher didn't even blink as he set down his empty bottle. JD had eaten most of what he'd taken, and that was most definitely a dismissal. He stood, having been brought up never to overstay his welcome. "I'm sorry you feel that way."

Fisher nodded slowly. "It really is better for you."

JD paused and walked over to where Fisher sat. He leaned down and kissed him on the cheek. "Are you sure it's me you're worried about?" He got his coat and gloves, then left the apartment. He walked down the steps, got in his car, and drove off and into the night, still trying to figure out what had happened.

"HI, UNCLE Jeffy," Alex said when Carter led JD inside the next afternoon. Alex practically jumped into his arms for a hug and then climbed down.

"Want a beer? It's a little early, but I think we earned it today," Carter said as he went into the kitchen and shared a kiss with Donald, who sat at the table in front of his computer, muttering under his breath.

"Maybe I should go," JD said.

Donald grumbled once again and then closed the lid on his laptop. "Don't mind me. The bureaucracy at work is driving me crazy, and I need to let it go." He stood and greeted JD with a hug. "What happened today that you need a beer at three in the afternoon?"

"There is some nasty sh… stuff going on," Carter answered. "Cocaine, meth, you name it. On the northeast quadrant, we got a call to what we thought was a domestic disturbance. Turned out two groups had moved into houses next door to each other. It started with yelling and ended as a gunfight between two rival drug gangs. They were taking shots at each other from the houses. You'd think we were in inner-city LA, not Carlisle. When we got back, the mayor called in the chief, and from the way he came back, the chief got reamed a new one, and now the chief is setting up a drug task force to try to figure out what the hell is happening."

"We thought it was someone moving into empty territory, but that doesn't seem to be it," JD interjected. The suspect who had tried to muscle Fisher had talked in exchange for a deal.

"It's a whole distribution system, probably because of the highway and the turnpike. This area is known for warehouses, so someone is setting up one for drugs. There are so many trucks, large and small, that they hide in the existing traffic." Carter opened two beers and handed one to JD. Alex came in with crayons and paper, then climbed into the chair next to JD and started to draw.

"What are you making?" Carter asked.

"I'm drawing Uncle Jeffy. He needs a picture for his house," Alex answered without looking up.

"He does?"

Alex nodded and kept working.

"How are things with your new friend?" Donald asked. "Did he find out anything about his job?"

"I don't know. I found him last night sitting on the square, and we had dinner at his house. It was a little strange. He got agitated about something that I'm still trying to figure out fully. I think it was the guy who broke into his building, which is a whole other thing, but I'm really not sure. He got very nervous, had to take some medication, and then basically said that it wasn't necessary for me to take pity on him and that it would probably be best for me if I left."

Donald nodded slowly and didn't look the least bit surprised.

"What?"

"He's had a traumatic brain injury, and he's bipolar because of it. That's a pretty knockout combination, and I suspect that's caused him a lot of heartache in relationships. It isn't unreasonable for him to want to protect himself from further pain."

"What? You're sitting there as though you know something and I'm the stupidest person on the planet." JD drank his beer and waited.

"Just tell him," Carter said.

Donald stuck out his tongue at Carter. "No tongue sticking," Alex scolded.

"That's right," Carter said in a superior tone.

Donald rolled his eyes and then turned to JD. "Did you and Fisher… do anything?"

"We kissed," JD admitted. He didn't like to kiss and tell.

"Ewww," Alex said. "Kissing is yucky."

"No, it's not," Donald told him. "Your papa and I kiss all the time, and it's not yucky."

"That's what you think," Alex responded, and they all broke into peals of laughter.

"Forgetting the philosophy of a five-year-old, maybe Fisher wasn't ready for it. Or it could be that he liked it too much," Donald said. "For guys like him, things need to move slowly and at a steady pace. Order, routine, and predictability are keys for him to stay level. It could be that he got overwhelmed between you, the kiss, his workplace burning down, the guy who broke into his building…. Think about it—that's a lot for anyone to take in one day, and he reacted by pulling back to where it was safe."

"That makes sense. So what should I do?" JD asked, taking another drink and then pushing the beer away. It wasn't settling well in his stomach.

"Do? There's nothing to do. He's a person who's most likely trying to live day-to-day and not fly apart."

Carter got up and lifted Alex into his arms. "Let's you and I let Daddy and Uncle Jeffy talk." He shifted Alex in his arms and zoomed him out of the room like an airplane. JD watched them go and then turned back to Donald.

"You really like him," Donald said.

"Yeah."

"So the kiss was good?" Donald asked. "Did things progress beyond kissing to copping a feel?"

"No. Well, not much. I held him and got to feel a little." JD stopped. Why did he feel like he was back in high school? Next they were going to talk about second and third base. "I like him," he said firmly, hopefully cutting off that line for discussion.

"Okay. Why?" Donald asked.

"I don't know. Why did you like Carter?" JD shot back. "I heard you two fought like cats and dogs at first, and that he used to call you Icicle. Why did you get together?"

Donald leaned closer. "Have you looked at him?" He got a dreamy, faraway look.

"Yeah, exactly. No reason other than he floated your boat," JD answered. "Why would it be any different for me and Fisher?"

"You just met him a few days ago. Give the guy some time and space. If things are meant to work out, they will. Carter and I were a disaster when we first met, and the second time it didn't go much better, but we were lucky. We had a three-year-old matchmaker who brought us together." Donald turned away from the peals of laughter coming from papa and son in the living room. JD had to admit he could think of few happier sounds. Without going to the bedroom, at least.

"JD, you also need to know that Fisher isn't going to change," Donald continued. "The issues he has are going to stay with him for the rest of his life. His memories won't return. He will have bipolar depression off and on as well as extreme mania. There isn't a cure. I'm sure he knows that—" Donald paused midsentence. "There's something else, isn't there?"

"Yeah." JD pulled back from the table. "I get it now. He was in an accident, and afterward his boyfriend left him for someone else. And he said he doesn't see his family." JD clenched his fist. "Everyone else pushed him away, so before it could happen again, he pushed me away."

"At least this way, he's in control," Donald said. "A lot of people with injuries like this lose control of their lives. Jobs are lost, families strained to the breaking point, homelessness, and worse. I see it all the time. Parents who self-medicate with anything they can find to keep the good times rolling and the depression at bay. It doesn't work and only makes things worse."

"But I don't want Fisher to be alone like that. He doesn't have to be."

"I know, but that's his choice, and you need to respect it." Donald leaned over the table. "If you want my advice, give him time, and if you run into each other again, let things flow at his pace. But you can't push it."

"All right. But I'm not exactly known for my patience, especially when I find something I want."

"Yeah. That tends to go with the territory. Carter isn't known for his patience either." Donald lowered his voice. "He can be downright pushy."

"I heard that," Carter called. "Daddy's picking on me."

Alex squealed and laughed, and JD stood up. "I should go and let the three of you have some family time. It doesn't look like there's going to be a lot of downtime for any of us in the near future, if the chief and mayor have their way." He hugged Donald and walked into the other room, thanked Carter for the beer, and left to begin the walk home.

It was still light out and a little warmer than it had been. When JD reached the square, he looked at the bench for Fisher, but it was empty.

Without thinking, he sat down, watching as people went by. He missed Fisher. Yeah, he knew it was dumb to miss someone he'd only met a few times, but he did. He had some friends and liked to think he'd been kind and tried to help Fisher by including him, but that was a lie. Yes, Fisher was alone, but not much more than JD was. Being with Fisher had been fun. They'd told stories—mostly depressing ones, but Fisher had become as indignant and sympathetic at JD's plight as JD had been for Fisher's, and they'd laughed together. It had been nice to make a new friend. Hell, it had been even nicer to kiss a man and have him return the heat without a boatload of guilt afterward.

JD sat back on the bench and realized that Fisher was exactly right. People walked past without seeing anyone. Just by sitting down and staying still, he'd become largely invisible. Lawyers hurried along the pathways on their way to their appointments in the courthouse across the street. Business owners went about their day. Exercisers power-walked among the war monuments and flower beds, and no one paid him the least bit of attention. JD didn't like the thoughts swirling around in his head. Being invisible sucked, and he hated that Fisher felt this way on a regular basis. He stood and strode away from the bench and out of the square, continuing down Hanover, choosing a route that wouldn't take him past Fisher's building on his way home.

CHAPTER *Four*

FISHER HUNG up the phone with a small sense of relief. For three days he'd called Optima each day to see what they planned to do, and finally today he'd gotten some news. They were renting warehouse space in the same complex on an emergency basis, and they expected that soon they would be calling people back to work. Fisher had been assured that they intended to pay their full-time employees for the week. At least that was one huge worry off his shoulders. He sat on his sofa and turned on the television. For three days he'd mostly sat, spending his days watching daytime television, and it was pretty dismal.

Normally he'd take a walk and probably spend some time sitting outside, but he was afraid to. He didn't want to admit it, but if he sat in the square or took a walk downtown, he was afraid one of the friends of the guy who had broken into his building and threatened him in his home might see him. He also might run into JD, and he wasn't sure he could face him. The following morning when he'd awakened, the entire conversation had replayed in his head. Sometimes when he took his meds it played with his memory, and he wasn't too sure what was real and what was his mind stringing things together, but his acting like a self-righteous pig to someone who had been nice to him had left Fisher cringing and feeling ashamed. That night, he'd spent a good share of it reliving the kisses he'd shared with JD, and his imagination had taken him on a flight of fancy that resulted in him getting out of bed to take a shower.

There was nothing to do about it now. He'd really messed things up with JD, just like he'd messed up the relationship with his family. Regardless of how he tried to think about it, the messes in his life were of his own making.

Fisher got off the sofa and walked to the window that overlooked the street. The sun shone, and it was warmer outside. There were plenty of people on the sidewalk and they seemed to be getting on okay. Fisher went to his closet and got a coat and a pair of sunglasses. Maybe he could hide behind them. When he was properly dressed, he left the apartment, locked his door, and then hurried down the stairs and out onto the sidewalk. The landlord had already had the front door repaired and strengthened. It made Fisher feel better that the landlord took the building's security seriously.

After taking a deep breath to steady his nerves, Fisher headed down the two commercial blocks of Pomfret, looking in the windows and taking in some fresh air. He'd brought his phone with him and felt it in his pocket. Not that he ever got any calls, but he needed to know it was there, just in case.

No one paid him any attention. He even checked behind him a few times, but of course no one was following him. He tried to push away the paranoid notion that he probably wouldn't know if they were. He was turning back around when he bumped full-on into someone. Fisher was lucky he didn't fall on his butt.

"Excuse me, I wasn't—"

Fisher turned and found himself staring into Gareth's eyes. He blinked and backed away. "Umm…." He wasn't sure what to say to him. "I need to be going."

"I haven't seen you around. How are you doing?" Gareth asked.

"I'm managing day-to-day." He thought that was a good answer.

"So things haven't gotten any better? I saw your mother last week, and she said you were still battling whatever demons you had. We talked, and she said she was trying to get you some professional help. Has she been in touch?"

"My injury left me with a permanent disability, Gareth," he said, stepping forward. "There's nothing I can do about it except learn to live within my abilities, take my medication, and try to be a good person and take care of myself. And I've done that without your help or that of my family. I've rebuilt my life as best I can. What have you done? Oh wait, you're still an asshole." He turned and strode toward the corner, making the turn and walking away as fast as he could.

Fisher could hardly believe he'd actually said that. For a second he was proud of himself for standing up to Gareth. Maybe he was getting over all that mess with the accident and putting it behind him.

"Fisher," Gareth yelled after him, and he picked up his pace, walking faster in time to his ever-increasing heartbeat. What if Gareth came after him? He walked even faster, not daring to look back.

"Oh my God," he whispered. Gareth had been talking to his mother. The two people who'd made his life a living hell were talking about him, comparing notes, deciding what they thought he needed. Fisher had been through all that and wasn't about to do it again. He gulped for air, now all but running. He reached the main street, checked for cars, and raced across. A horn blared behind him, but he continued on. If Gareth was after him, that should slow him down. Fisher didn't stop or pause to check; he looked ahead, watching for people coming toward him. His feet and legs tingled and his hands shook, but he didn't dare stop. He was not going back to some hospital where he had no say or control over anything in his life. No way, no how. He shook his head wildly to punctuate his own thoughts and continued running, getting the hell away from whatever was chasing him.

Slowly, reality and realization trickled around the edges of his mind, growing stronger, and Fisher slowed, then stopped, bending over to get air into his burning lungs. "I'm okay," he whispered over and over. "I'm fine. There's no one behind me. It was just a panic attack, and it's over. It doesn't matter what Gareth says. He's a jackass, and I don't need to listen to him. I'm safe, and he can't hurt me ever again." He kept repeating the sentiments like a mantra, over and over, adding others until he could stand up.

Fisher didn't know where he was. None of the houses or streets looked familiar. He tried to think where he was and what had happened, but his memory was fuzzy and he wasn't sure how he'd gotten here. A sharp sound split the air, and Fisher stood stock-still wondering what exactly had happened. A man barreled toward him, his face obscured by the hood of his gray sweatshirt. Fisher jumped out of the way as another man, this one wearing a navy blue hoodie, raced after him.

"Son of a bitch, you're dead," the man in the blue hoodie screamed, both of them running as though the hounds of hell were after them. A shot rang out, and then another. Fisher jumped into a yard and fell to the ground, covering his head with his arms, shaking like a leaf. He didn't look up from the ground, whimpering and moaning, rocking from side to side, anything to keep his head from exploding. Leaves pressed to his face, and he inhaled dust and dirt, which brought on coughing, but he was too scared to look at anything.

An ache in his side got his attention. At first he wondered if he'd been shot, but it was his phone digging into his hip. He pulled it out, hoping it wasn't broken, and redialed the last number called. "Help me," he whispered when he heard a voice on the other end. "I don't know where I am, just help me." Fisher dropped the phone on the ground and kept his head covered, wondering if the men who'd been running would come back for him.

Quiet seeped into Fisher's mind. There were no footsteps, no shots, just the wind rustling dry leaves. Still, he didn't dare move.

"Fisher."

He jumped and recoiled when someone touched him. "Don't hurt me," he cried, begged, heck, he didn't know what he was doing. The words were out before he could think. "Just don't hurt me. I didn't see anything. I...."

"Fisher, it's me. JD."

He lifted his head off the leaves. "What?"

"You called me. God, I had a hard time finding you." JD helped him sit up and then pulled him into a hug. "You're all right. Did you get hurt? What happened?" He paused a second, then said into his radio, "Red, I found him in the avenues, near D and College."

"They... I...." Fisher didn't know where to begin as tears welled. He buried his face in JD's shoulder and began to cry. It had been a long time since he'd shed tears, but he was so confused, and as the fear leached away it had to be replaced, and that was all he had.

"Take your time," JD said, staying where he was.

"I saw men running, one chasing the other. Maybe shots. I'm not sure," Fisher said, wiping his eyes.

"What are you doing way up here? Did you walk all this way?"

"I think so," Fisher answered. "I must have, but I don't remember it all, exactly. I saw Gareth, and he was mean and yelled after me. I wanted to get away, so I kept going. Then men started running toward me. I think I heard shots, and I stayed on the ground until you got here."

Sirens sounded and Fisher tensed.

"It's only Red," JD said. "There have been reports of shots in this area, so we were investigating, and then you called. We were able to trace your call, but only to the area of town."

"It was definitely gunshots," Red said as he got out of his car and approached where Fisher still sat on the ground. "Were you hit?"

"No. But I might have seen the man who was shooting. I'm just not sure." Fisher tried to calm himself and put his thoughts and memories in order. "A man in jeans and a gray hoodie ran toward me, with another man after him yelling that he was dead." Fisher kept his voice as level as he could, but his panic began to rise again just by recounting what had happened.

"I'll call all this in," Red said. "We're going to need to get people over here to canvass the neighborhood and see if we can find anything."

Fisher swallowed, bile rising in his throat. "They went that way. The first shots came from over there, and the last ones from where they went. I didn't see anything else."

"Thanks," Red said and began contacting people on his radio. Soon other sirens sounded in the distance, getting louder. JD helped him to his feet and opened the back door of his cruiser, giving him a place to sit.

"Just relax and breathe. Do you want me to call an ambulance? You're still flushed and breathing hard."

"I'll be okay," he said. He wasn't as afraid, and now that he'd said what he could, he closed his eyes and let JD take over. When the other cars arrived, the officers conferred out of his hearing, and then he watched as they fanned out.

"Do you need someone to take you home?" The voice was strange, and he lifted his gaze. "I'm Detective Cloud. Officer Burnside has some tasks he has to do. He'll be back in a little while, and if you can wait, he'll take you home."

"Thanks. I'd appreciate that."

"Did you see who fired any of the shots?" he asked.

"No. I heard them and saw men running, but that was all. I told Red and JD what I saw, and they wrote it down."

"Do you live near here?"

"No. I live on Pomfret," he answered.

"Then what were you doing all the way out here without a car?" the detective asked forcefully.

"I was walking." Fisher's stomach began to clench and the calm that had begun to settle in was shattered. "I went for a walk and got... turned around." He tried to think of how he could explain everything without sounding as crazy as his family and Gareth seemed to think he was. God, why had he stepped outside his apartment? After seeing Gareth, he should have gone home, locked his door, and stayed there. The detective was looking at him like he was either a freak or he had something to do with whatever had happened out here.

"That's quite a distance," Detective Cloud said.

"Aaron," JD called as he approached, and Fisher sighed with relief as the detective stepped away. He and JD spoke quietly, and then the detective nodded to him and turned to the other officers. "Come on," JD said. "My shift is over, and Aaron said I should take you home." Fisher got in the front seat, and JD closed the door. Then he got in and began the drive through town.

"He thought I was involved with the shooting," Fisher said.

"It's his job to ask questions and try to get to the bottom of what happened. He's a suspicious man but very good at his job. I explained what had happened and why you were there. I also told him that I knew you, and it helped that we found some shell casings and other evidence."

Fisher didn't ask what it was. He didn't want to think about blood trails or dead bodies at the moment. They took a back way, and soon JD pulled into the station. "I need to get my things, and then I'll take you home in my car." They got out, and Fisher went inside, sitting in the lobby area while JD did what he needed to do.

Officers went about their business, but whenever one of them looked at him, or walked his way, Fisher half expected them to take him back to one of those little rooms they probably had so they could ask him more questions.

"Let's go," JD said as he approached, and Fisher stood, left the station with him, and got into JD's car. He expected to be taken to his apartment, so he was surprised when JD pulled up in front of a small house.

"Where are we?"

"This is my place. I don't think you should be alone right now. You need time to settle down." JD got out, then hurried around and opened his door. "Just come in for a while."

"I don't need you to take care of me," Fisher protested. His legs started tingling again as his anxiety rose, and when he took a step, his left leg buckled under him. JD caught him and half carried Fisher to the front door. Once Fisher managed to stand, JD got them inside and helped Fisher over to the sofa.

"I'll get you some water, and you can settle down. There's nothing to be nervous about. I have some crackers and cheese and fruit if you need something to eat." JD hurried out of the room and came back with a bottle of water. Fisher stared at it. "It's me," JD said, and Fisher nodded, blankly taking the bottle. "You're worrying me."

"I'm okay. Just a little worn-out and confused. I need a chance to think about what happened and...." Fisher raised his gaze, thankful when JD sat in a chair close by. He needed quiet and calm, not JD running around and adding to his worry.

"What happened with Gareth? What did he say to you?" JD asked.

"That he talked to my mother and that they wanted me to get some help." Fisher opened the bottle of water. "The last time my mother decided I needed help, she tried to put me in a private hospital. I guess they told her they could make me well. I fought her and she couldn't do anything about it. I have a right to make my own decisions. So when I told my mom I didn't want to be hospitalized, she turned her back on me, and Gareth told me she said she was going to try again." At least that's what Fisher had heard Gareth say, and he wasn't going to allow that to happen.

"I hope you told Gareth off," JD said.

Fisher began to giggle. "I did. I told him I had a mental illness, but he was still an asshole." He drank from the bottle. "But then he yelled at me, and I thought he might come after me, so I walked faster. I wasn't sure if he was still behind me, so I kept going, and then I was in a strange place and got a panic attack. And then the men started running at me, yelling, and then I heard shots and dove onto the ground. I hurt my hip, but it reminded me I had my phone with me, so I called you." He inhaled and drank some more water. "That's all there is to it." He tried to stop his hand from shaking.

"Just try to relax."

"I was, and then you left me with that detective person, and he started questioning me and acting like I was the one doing the shooting. Don't police officers have bedside manner, or witness-side manner, or something like that?" God, he was ramping up, and his mouth didn't want to turn off.

"I'm afraid not. Sometimes we get more answers when we ask pushy questions. It comes with the job." JD left the room again. Fisher took off his coat and sat back, looking around at the odd collection of things. Fisher knew he was pretty anal about keeping his apartment clean. JD didn't seem to have that same compunction. Not that the house was dirty, just a little untidy. Though once again, that could be his analness coming out. Most people probably would have thought the place was very nice, but Fisher could see a light coating of dust under JD's chair and wondered if JD would have a fit if he got something to wipe it up.

JD returned with a plate of cheese and some crackers that he put on the table. Fisher reached for them and nibbled on them, then drank more water. At least he had something to do.

"Do you get these kinds of attacks often?" JD asked.

"No. I had a few of them before the doctors put me on this medication and got it regulated. They're bipolar panic attacks, and it just takes over. The first time I had one, I thought I was hearing voices and wondered why I couldn't understand what people were saying. I actually thought that God was speaking to me, and yet at the same time, I knew he wasn't. But then they put me on medication, and we began working to get the right doses and stuff." He paused and realized he was running on again. "It's been a few years, and I wish I knew why this one happened." He huffed and blew air upward so it caught his front cowlick. "The last one was two years ago, and before you ask, I did take my medication."

"Hey. I wasn't going to ask, and I'm glad you're feeling better."

Fisher nodded, sinking gratefully into the sofa cushions and letting the comfort surround him. He took deep breaths and tried to settle his mind on one subject. When he opened his eyes, JD was looking back at him with a goofy smile, so he concentrated on that and found he was smiling back. "What?" he finally asked.

"Nothing. I just wasn't expecting to see you again after the last time, and then you called me."

Fisher felt his hand shake and set the water on a coaster. "I'm sorry about that. I know it isn't an excuse, but there are times when I overreact to things and—"

JD got up and sat next to him on the sofa. "It's okay. I was going too fast."

"It wasn't that. People have pushed me away, and I guess I pushed you away first, before you could do it." He reached for his water, but JD took his hand instead. "Look. I'm pretty messed up, as you saw today. I don't handle stress very well, or surprises, and what 'normal' people see and process overwhelms me." That was the easiest way to try to explain it. The truth was that things happened and sometimes he reacted without really knowing why. Fisher could see that he was doing something or hear his own words, but they had a power of their own. He'd even want to stop what he was doing or saying, but he couldn't. Sometimes it was like watching a movie of himself driving off a cliff, unable to do anything about it. "I really appreciate that you're being nice to me. I do, and I can't tell you what it meant that you came when I called."

"Of course I did. I told you if you needed anything to call me."

"But I was such a jerk."

JD held his hand tighter, and Fisher liked it. He wasn't hurting him, but his grip was solid and steady. "How about we put that behind us? Just promise me that if you're going to try to be proactive about something, like, I don't know, pushing me away for my own good or because you're afraid of something, you'll talk to me."

"But sometimes things… take over."

"Talking about things can help."

Fisher turned and looked deeply into JD's intensely blue eyes. "Gosh, you're beautiful," he said. "Why would you want a messed-up, crazy person like me in your life?"

JD grinned, showing perfect white teeth. "How about we just say that I have a thing for rugged blonds with ocean-blue eyes and pouty lips." JD ran his hands through Fisher's hair and trailed his fingers along his jaw. "You have no idea how handsome you are." JD leaned closer. "And I love that you have dimples when you smile."

"I do not." Fisher tried not to smile and failed miserably.

JD leaned back and whooped softly.

"What was that for?"

"I got you to smile. I feel like spiking the football and doing one of those touchdown chicken dances in the end zone."

"Now that I'd like to see," Fisher said, watching to see if JD was actually going to flap his arms and legs after spiking an imaginary ball. He didn't. Instead, he leaned closer, the tilt slipping from his lips.

"How about feel?"

"JD. This is where things went wrong the last time."

"Kissing was wrong?"

"No. But you started moving quickly, and...."

JD wasn't moving back. He just stayed still, blinking. "You didn't like when I kissed you?"

"Of course I liked it. You're a really good kisser, but...."

Danged if JD didn't move closer, and Fisher's nose filled with musk and a hint of sweat, perfume of the gods. "Then enjoy it. Just be happy and allow yourself a little fun and pleasure in the moment. Not everything is earth-shattering. Sometimes a kiss, or a touch"—JD put his hand on Fisher's, surrounding it in warmth—"is just two people saying hello... with possibilities." JD closed the gap between them.

Heat instantly flared through Fisher, and before he knew it, he'd slid his arms around JD's neck, his hands and arms tickled by his hair. This was nice—no, more than nice, inspiring—and it made him want things he didn't think he could have. When JD wrapped his arms around Fisher's waist and tugged him closer, for a few seconds the anxiety and voices of caution in his head grew silent. All that existed was JD's mouth on his, the way he parted his lips and used his tongue to lightly flick along the edge of Fisher's bottom teeth. A soft moan floated through the room, and Fisher realized it had come from him.

"See, you can allow yourself to be happy."

"This isn't one of those touchdown, chicken-dance times, is it?" Fisher asked.

JD shook his head from side to side only once, locking their gazes together, and then he cupped Fisher's jaw in his hand, guiding their lips back together. When JD pulled back a little bit later, Fisher was flushed, sweating a little, and his blood pounded in his ears. He didn't want this to end. He felt alive and whole, at least for a short time. He could imagine that there was nothing wrong with him, and that JD could want him and be happy with him.

"Don't move," JD whispered. "Whatever has you looking as though you're about to jump into a pool of whipped cream, hold on to that, store it away, and bring it out again when things get difficult."

"Is that how you do it?"

"Yeah, only I'm going to hold on to that look on your face, right now." JD traced his thumb over Fisher's lips, and danged if he didn't yawn. Fisher tried to stop it, but failed.

"You've been through a lot in the past few hours. If you need to rest, I have a guest room where you can lie down." JD jumped up and hurried out of the room. He returned with a blanket and set it on the sofa next to him.

"I'm okay," Fisher said as his mouth betrayed him again. JD gathered up the dishes and glasses, leaving Fisher alone in the living room. He took the blanket and stretched out on the sofa, surprised at how comfortable it was. He really should go home, but being with someone was nice, and he felt safer. Fisher checked the time and remembered he needed to take his pills. So he got up and fished out the travel container he carried with him. He went to the downstairs bathroom and took his pills, then returned to the sofa.

"Is that good?" JD asked, turning out the light in the room. Before Fisher could answer, the doorbell rang and JD left the room. Fisher settled down and listened as JD opened the door and spoke softly to someone. He heard the door slide closed and followed JD with his gaze as he carried a large envelope through the room to the kitchen.

Fisher was curious. He had no right to ask what it was, of course, but big envelopes in his experience rarely brought good news. Big envelopes contained restraining orders telling him to stay away from the home he grew up in. Fisher put that out of his head as best he could. He was being silly. It was only a package that JD had received, nothing more.

"Dammit," Fisher heard JD breathe from the kitchen. He opened his eyes and looked through to the other room, but he couldn't see JD. He pushed back the covers and stood, then approached slowly until he saw JD sitting at the table, papers in front of him, holding his head in his hands. Fisher knew that "what am I going to do" stance all too well.

"Are you okay?"

JD lifted his gaze, and Fisher didn't know what to make of his expression. "It's from a lawyer in Charleston about Aunt Lillibeth. She left me her estate. All of it."

"What about your dad?" Fisher asked.

"She says in the will that he has plenty of his own and doesn't need anything from her, and that she doesn't want my mother to get her claws into anything of hers. I guess my aunt had some claws of her own." JD looked back down at the papers. "I didn't even go back for the funeral. I let my mother guilt me into staying here instead of telling them all to fuck off and doing what I knew was right." JD gasped.

"Is that bad?"

"No. I don't know what it all means. There are listings for offshore holdings, her house, and a beach house, as well as artwork and cars."

"Was your aunt loaded?" Fisher asked.

"I don't know. I mean, I know about the house she lived in. It was nice—very old, and not huge or anything. And I used to visit her at the beach, but I didn't know she owned the house there. I thought it was a rental she got every year." He didn't move, still staring at the papers in front of him.

Fisher went up behind JD and gently rested his hands on his shoulders. He slowly kneaded his fingers into JD's neck. Tension that hadn't been there ten minutes earlier now filled the room, and Fisher could almost feel the presence of the specter of guilt forming in the corner and then getting larger until it loomed over them like a giant bear ready to strike.

"What should I do? I don't deserve any of this. I didn't even go back for her funeral because...." JD didn't finish his thought.

"You were scared?" Fisher supplied. "I know all about being afraid of shit. I live my life in a state of nervous anxiety wondering what bad thing is going to happen to me next, and the worst thing is that bad stuff does happen."

"But it's not necessarily your fault," JD said. "I did this. I let my mother talk me out of doing what I knew was right and look at me. I stayed away from the funeral of the one person in my family who didn't turn her back on me." He turned, and Fisher's hands fell to his side. "For what? To make people happy who will never accept me or want me back in their lives again? Why did I care what they thought?"

"Because you didn't want a fight at your aunt's funeral. Besides, your aunt was gone. She wasn't there. It was just her body, and all that funeral stuff is for the living. The person in the casket only lives on inside of us, in our hearts." Fisher pulled out the chair next to JD's and sat down. "If your aunt is looking down on you, then she understands the things that happened with your family, and she isn't going to hold it against you."

JD turned his attention away from the papers. "Aunt Lillibeth always knew her own mind, and whatever she wanted, she did. And she could get under my mother's skin faster than anyone... ever."

"So she didn't like your mother?"

"No."

"Then she isn't going to blame you. I wouldn't blame you."

JD looked up at him, eyes warming. "Is there anyone in your family that you still see?"

"No. Everyone in my family has to get around or through my mother, including my dad. They won't stand up to her."

"Why? Not that I stood up to my own mother."

"Mom has the money in my family, and a lot of it. My father has ridden her coattails for their entire marriage, and my younger brother doesn't want to be cut out or off, so he stays quiet and out of the way. My sisters are all their mother's daughters. Mom runs things, and anyone in her sphere either gets with her or gets out of the way. After my accident, my mom wanted to run everything in my life, and when I was having issues that wouldn't go away and might be embarrassing, she wanted to get me out of sight."

"It seems our mothers have a lot in common." JD picked up the papers and began sliding them back into the envelope. "Weren't you tired?"

"I was. But you were upset, so…."

"Go on and lie down if you want. You were right. I was upset over something I can't change, and my aunt would be pissed at me if I let my mother get to me. If I know my aunt, she left me her estate so I could be free from my mother if that was what I wanted."

"And do you?" Fisher asked.

"More than anything. Well, more than almost anything."

Something in JD's voice sent a chill followed by a flush of heat racing up Fisher's back. He shifted back and forth as the sensation shimmied up his back like the fluid flip of a dolphin's tail. He wasn't even sure exactly what JD meant, but he was pretty sure, especially given the way he didn't look away, that JD was referring to him.

Truthfully, Fisher wasn't sure how he felt about being the object of JD's attention. It was nice, but the relationships he'd had, both romantic and otherwise, hadn't survived his accident and its aftermath. What if JD realized that Fisher wasn't worth the trouble the way everyone else had? "JD."

"I know. I need to slow down and let you catch up."

He wasn't sure if he cared for that. "You make me sound like I'm some broken-down horse that everyone needs to wait for to cross the finish line."

"No." JD pulled at his collar. "I talked to Donald a few days ago. He said that your life is built around routine and things that are familiar. He said a lot of other stuff too, but I think the point was that I need to become a part of your routine instead of trying to upset it."

Fisher stood and went back to the sofa, needing a minute to process how he felt about JD talking to Donald about him.

"It wasn't anything bad, I promise. I needed his advice after the way you acted because I was hurt and surprised. He gave me a little insight and told me I needed to be patient."

"But how did you know I'd call you?" Fisher asked as he sat and pulled the blanket over his legs. JD sat next to him and spread the fabric over his own legs as well.

"I didn't. All I could do was hope that our paths would cross again. I didn't expect it to be at the scene of a shooting, but I was pleased—for a few seconds, anyway—when your number displayed on my phone. I did tell myself, though, that if I got a second chance, I was going to try to make the most of it. So I'll try to go at your pace and let you guide me. I'm not a patient person, but I will try to be patient with you."

"You talked to other people about me?" Fisher was having a hard time letting that go.

"If I didn't care, I wouldn't have talked to him."

"Okay." He would try to accept that. "Oh, I should tell you that I start back to work on Monday. I finally got an answer. They think they will have the systems restored and cleared out. We'll have to put in all the bin information, and then we can start receiving shipments."

"Will you help with this bin information? I don't really know what that is, but it sounds like progress."

"Yeah. They said that they have temporary space and that the plan is to rebuild the warehouse on the land we have. So at least my job is going to stay." That had been a huge load off his mind.

"One less stress inducer," JD said, and Fisher couldn't disagree with that. "Come here." JD tugged him into another kiss, and this time Fisher let go of his baggage and went with it.

"I like kissing you," Fisher said when they came up for air.

JD pantomimed being disappointed. "Just *like* it? I'll have you know that I've spent much toil and work to perfect my kissing skills."

"Exactly how much of this work and toil did you expend, and where are all these men you've been kissing?" He tried to keep the same teasing tone JD had used, but jealousy rose from deep in his gut. He didn't like the idea of JD kissing other people, not at all. "I hope this isn't a recent journey of discovery and self-improvement."

"No. I did my studies quite a while ago and haven't been able to put my theoretical knowledge to practical use in quite some time."

"Good," Fisher said as he closed the gap between them. He felt a little like a teenager making out on his parents' sofa, except, well, he'd never made out with anyone anywhere near his mother's precious, delicate, "don't sit there" furniture.

After a few minutes of kissing, Fisher, hoping it was okay, let his fingers do a little roaming under the blankets. JD's legs were large, stretching his jeans, muscles quivering under his hand. As he continued, Fisher encountered a sizable bulge, and JD closed his eyes, groaning slightly. Dang, he hadn't meant to be a tease, and he pulled his hand away, but he wished he'd done a little more exploring first.

JD pulled them together, and Fisher pressed his hand to JD's chest to steady himself. "Are you made of rocks?" he muttered as he patted JD's chest. "Nice rocks. Hot rocks." He ended up with his hand under JD's shirt and…. "Rub on you until my head explodes rocks."

"Honey, you can do whatever you want. I work out a lot because keeping in top physical condition is part of my job, and it means that I can better protect myself and the public." JD sounded like he was the spokesman in an infomercial.

"You work out because you like how it makes you look," Fisher said. "There's nothing wrong with that. I like how you look." He snuggled closer as JD wrapped his arms around him.

"But I do need to stay in shape for my job."

"Yeah, but that's not the only reason you do it." He rested his head on JD's bulging shoulder until JD's phone rang. "Dang it."

"I hope it's not work." JD reached for his phone, groaning.

"I can go home if you need me to," Fisher said, pushing back the blanket to get to his feet.

"Speak of the devil." JD showed him the display, which read "Mom," and then he answered the phone. "I'm a little busy at the moment," he said into phone. "I did what you asked and stayed away. Now I want you to leave me alone to grieve in my own way for a while." He paused a second. "I have company at the moment. You can call me later." JD hung up the phone, looking like the cat that just ate the canary. "That felt good."

"You could have taken the call. What if it was important?" Fisher asked with concern.

"There isn't anything that could be that important, and she always expects everyone to drop what they're doing because she crooks her finger. My mom turned her back on her own son, so she doesn't deserve to be a priority." He got up and wandered over to the front windows. "It's nice outside."

"Do you want to do something?" Fisher asked.

"We could drive out to the antique stores on the pike. There are a few nice ones out there, and I need to get a shade for a lamp I found at Goodwill. I've been meaning to have a look around but haven't had a chance." JD let the curtains fall back. "We'll drive, of course."

"If that's what you want." An attack like the one he'd had usually sapped all his energy out of him. When JD had suggested he lie down, it had been a good idea, and if it had stayed quiet, he'd have dropped off. But JD had so much energy, and Fisher didn't want to sleep through their time together. He could go to bed early and sleep late because he didn't have to go to work. "One of the shops out there has a game room with pinball machines."

"Oh, I love those."

"Me too. I'm really good," Fisher boasted.

"You brave enough to take on the master?" JD puffed out his ample chest. "Then let's go, and we can see who the pinball wizard is." He got a coat and handed Fisher his coat, and then they left the house.

The ride went quickly, and they stopped at the first store they came to. It had been there for many years and was filled with the sorts of things his grandmother had thrown away. A lot of items were broken and in poor condition. This seemed to be where undesired collectibles went to die. At least that was Fisher's initial impression. He looked at the first cases and wandered on, not paying much attention to the items because nothing really caught his eye.

"This is nice," JD said.

Fisher retraced his few steps to where JD was looking. "That's a reproduction, probably made last year. They fool people," Fisher said, marveling as JD turned to him skeptically. "And you're the police officer. These Chinese vases have been very popular and desirable for a while, and when that happens, people recreate them. Some are good and others… less good." Fisher picked up the vase. "This is a decent one, but…." He turned it over. "The clay is too white and the wear too even. Even the mark is close, but no cigar." Fisher put the vase back on the shelf.

"How do you know?"

"Years of watching *Antiques Roadshow*, reading books, and some experience." He continued walking down the rows, past a case of vintage Halloween decorations. "Also, if it sounds too good to be true, then it probably is." Especially in a place like this. Fisher didn't say that out loud, but he definitely thought it. While it was possible to find a real gem among chipped pieces of Fiestaware and Depression glass, it wasn't likely.

"An old fire hydrant," JD said as he nearly tripped over one with the last bits of red paint clinging to it.

"Sure. They make great yard decorations," Fisher said. "Almost anything can make its way here."

"No kidding," JD said. "I've only driven by these places, and I thought since you had some antiques that you might like it. I didn't know you were an expert."

"I'm not. But you have to know what you have and develop some basic knowledge of what things are." Fisher picked up a silver creamer from a set.

"Silver plate," JD said.

"Yes, but look where the silver is worn on the bottom of the legs. It's not gray, but copper. That's an indication of Sheffield silver and real quality." He set the creamer back on the tray. "This may be the hidden gem in this whole place, and everyone walks right by it because it's black and dirty." Fisher continued on to the back, and then they made their way up the store and toward the checkout counter.

"What is it?" JD asked from behind him. Fisher hadn't even realized that he'd stopped and was standing stock-still. "Fisher...," he whispered.

"That's...." He made his legs work and turned to the back of the store again. "That's Gareth's new boyfriend behind the counter. At least it's the man I saw Gareth with a while ago."

"Do you want to leave?" JD asked.

Fisher took a deep breath, wishing air were whiskey for a few seconds. "No. I'm fine."

"It's okay to be upset."

"No, it's not." Fisher straightened his back and wiped the familiar sense of loss that threatened to spill from his eyes. "I wasn't worth it for Gareth to hold on to after my accident, so maybe when this man does something Gareth doesn't like, he'll find himself on the outside looking in as well." He returned to the tea set and checked the price. Then he made up his mind and lifted the tray and its contents. "How can I go wrong for thirty bucks?"

"But what will you do with it?" JD asked.

"I'm not sure," Fisher answered, walking back up toward the checkout desk. As he approached, a man came inside and walked right up, stepping in front of Fisher. "I called about the cloisonné vase. You were holding it behind the counter for me. The name was Spencer."

Fisher set the tray on the edge and stepped back, letting the man get what he wanted.

"Of course," Gareth's boyfriend said with a smile that was too big. He retrieved a large cloisonné vase and placed it in a bag. The man paid for it and got a receipt before leaving the store.

"Even he seems like he's in a rush to get out of here." There were no windows, and Fisher was already beginning to feel closed in. The store smelled musty, but not in a good way. Maybe moldy was a better description, like the building was decaying along with its contents.

"Did you find everything okay?" Gareth's boyfriend said.

"Yes. I was wondering if you could take twenty for this," Fisher asked. *Always bargain in places like this.* Gareth's boyfriend didn't seem to recognize him, and after a few seconds, he agreed to the price and rang it up. Once he was done, he wrapped the pieces in tissue and then put them in a shopping bag and handed it to Fisher. "Thanks for stopping in," he said.

"Thank you," Fisher said, and they left the store. JD unlocked the car, and Fisher put his purchase on the floor of the backseat.

"Did that seem strange to you?" JD asked.

"What?" Fisher turned in the seat.

"Nothing," JD said. "It's just me being a cop." He started the engine and backed out of the lot before heading down the pike.

At their next stop, they wandered the booths without finding anything and completed their visit in the arcade. A dozen vintage pinball machines lined the back wall. Fisher loved them and wished he had the room to buy one and put it in his apartment. "A man in Newville buys and restores them." He walked up to a space-themed machine and started it. "That's the cool part—no quarters required." He played a game and then stepped back to let JD have a turn. They ended up laughing and having a good time.

Fisher forgot about the challenge until JD brought it up and proceeded to clean his clock. The balls went everywhere JD seemed to want them to go, but Fisher had nothing but bad luck.

"So what's my prize?" JD asked.

"Dinner?" Fisher offered as JD's phone rang. JD nodded as he pulled it out of his pocket. It must have been his mother, because he had an expression identical to the last time she'd called.

"What is it, Mother?" he asked with a disinterested sigh, and Fisher felt his heated gaze still on him. "Yes." JD stiffened and the bemused expression fell from his face. "You will not." He listened, and Fisher stepped closer at the distress in his voice. "There is no basis, and you know it. She made it perfectly clear what she wanted." JD listened, then jabbed at his phone and shoved it back into his pocket.

"What is it?"

JD shook his head and walked toward the door. The fun portion of the day seemed to have ended, just like that. Fisher followed JD out to the car, and they got in.

JD gripped the steering wheel, knuckles bone white as he tried to tear the steering column from the car as he pulled on the wheel. "She says she's going to contest my aunt's will, and worse, that she's getting on a plane and will be arriving tomorrow so we can talk about this."

"Tell her to go away. You don't have to see her, you know that," Fisher said. He knew it was true, but he also knew that if his own mother were to call and tell him she was coming over, the old childhood programming would kick in and he'd welcome her, even knowing the visit would likely result in heartache and anger.

"Yeah, I do." JD unclenched his fingers. "She wants something from me, and she's using this will to try to get it. The only way I'm going to find out is by allowing a visit from my barracuda of a mother."

"I'll be there with you if you want," Fisher offered. "She isn't as likely to be as mean if there's someone else around. I also have some experience with sharklike mothers."

"Are you sure? She said she had already booked a flight and would be here tomorrow afternoon. So I get to work all morning keeping the streets safe from predators only to spend the afternoon and evening with one in my own house."

"Maybe you can talk her out of it," Fisher said. "If the will is legal, there isn't much she can do. Your aunt had to have a lawyer draw up the will, so contact him and tell him what your mother is planning to do. You don't have to do this all alone. Get people who can help you." Fisher touched JD's arm. "I'll help you. I don't know what I can do other than be there or listen, but I'll do what I can." JD had been nice to him, and Fisher figured he could do what he could in return.

"Thanks. But you don't need to get involved in my family mess."

"If you don't want help, that's fine." Fisher couldn't keep the hurt out of his voice even though he didn't have a reason to be hurt and he knew it. This was family stuff, and maybe JD didn't want an outsider hearing his private business.

"It's just that my mother…. You don't need to be exposed to my mother."

"You make her sound like a disease," Fisher observed.

JD scoffed and started the engine. "That's not a bad description, actually. My mother, the disease. Let's see, the symptoms she causes are massive indigestion, gastric distress, heart palpitations, with occasional ball-busting pain. Yeah, I think I'd want to keep her quarantined so as few of my friends as possible are exposed to her."

"But sometimes there's safety in numbers, and it's nice not being alone." He sat quietly while JD drove, anger and tension rolling off him. "If the roles were reversed, and it was my mother pushing her way into my life, would you offer to be there for me?" This question was so telling for Fisher.

JD's arms lost some of their rigidity and the tension lessened. "You know I would."

"Then how can you expect me not to be there for you? That is, unless this is some pity thing on your part." He was pushing it, but Fisher had to know if JD really thought he was someone worth kissing, and doing other things with, or if JD saw him as some pathetic person that he felt sorry for.

"This isn't a pity thing." JD turned onto Pomfret and pulled to a stop in front of Fisher's apartment building.

"Then you see me as an equal? Or am I a broken person who can't be a part of the things that happen in your life? You can't have it both ways, JD."

"I know. But my mother can be cruel, and when she doesn't get her own way, she tends to fight dirty and no-holds-barred. Never physically, but she'll use whatever she can find to hurt and consequently wear you out until you simply give up out of exhaustion."

"She doesn't have anything on me and doesn't know who I am. So she can swing away all she wants. But if you're not alone, then maybe she won't fight as dirty." Fisher got out of the car, got his bag from the back, and waited for JD. At first he wondered if JD was going to just go home. However, he opened his door and got out, joining Fisher on the sidewalk.

"I think it would be very nice if you joined us tomorrow." The formality in JD's voice threw him off for a second. "Just know that my mother isn't used to being thwarted, and knowing me, I'm likely to stand in her way just on principle."

"I understand," Fisher said. He unlocked the door and let them inside and up to his place. He felt like he'd won some sort of small victory. But he still wasn't sure exactly how JD saw him, or maybe the issue was with how he saw himself. Sometimes he felt like an angsty teenager going from lows to highs and then back down to new lows of self-doubt and insecurity.

"I don't you think you do," JD said from behind him as they climbed the stairs. "What you said was right. I don't have to do this alone. I have friends who care about me and will stand behind me. I need to stop thinking that my mother will run everyone off. And I need to remember that no matter what she feels or how uncomfortable seeing me with you will be, she's the one with the problem, not me, and I'm not going to change my life to suit her." With each declaration, JD's voice got louder.

Fisher unlocked his door and got them inside before the entire building heard what they were talking about. "You're a police officer. You handle criminals and bad people every day."

"Yet I can't handle my mother," JD groused and flopped down on the sofa.

Fisher took off his coat and hung up both his and JD's, then put away his purchase before sitting next to JD on the sofa. "I'd rather handle eighteen badass, 'been on the road for twelve hours' truckers than deal with my mother any day of the week," he admitted.

"Amen to that," JD said as he took Fisher's hand. "God, I just want to forget about mothers, wills...."

"...being chased and scared out of my mind," Fisher added.

JD nodded his agreement and cupped Fisher's cheeks, guiding him close. "This is the best way I know of to forget. Replace the bad thoughts with something very good." The intensity in JD's eyes burned into him, and Fisher didn't hesitate. His pulse raced and his heart pounded. He'd had so many ups and downs that his body seemed primed for action, and JD's proximity and energy was like adding gasoline to a forest fire. He pushed forward, capturing JD's lips and pressing him back on the sofa.

"Man," JD moaned softly, and Fisher pulled away, staring into his eyes, wondering if he'd done something wrong. "I expected you to be cautious."

For a second Fisher considered backing off, but he liked being in charge. It gave him a sense of control, something that he didn't have over many things in his life. When he kissed JD again, ignoring his comment, JD wrapped him in his arms and held him close on top of his large, strong body. Damn, it was hot feeling JD's strength under him, knowing JD could turn the tables whenever he wanted and yet he let Fisher do the driving.

"Dang, you're like a furnace," Fisher said, tugging at the hem of JD's shirt, and after some squirming on JD's part, Fisher tossed it to the floor, marveling at JD's sculpted chest and belly. He looked his fill, wanting to see, feel, and taste all of him at once. JD tugged open Fisher's shirt and slid the fabric down his arms.

Fisher wanted to turn away. He was skinny, too skinny, and he wondered what JD would think. When he forced his gaze back to JD's, what he saw was heat and lust burning openly. He almost turned to see if there was someone else behind him. "How can you look at me like that?"

"Like what?" JD asked, trailing his fingers down Fisher's chest, flicking one of his nipples until Fisher squirmed at the sensation.

"Like I'm lunch and you're starving to death," Fisher answered as JD pulled him closer, until they were chest to chest and JD's heat seared against Fisher's skin. He closed his eyes and took it in.

"That's because you are. You're beautiful, lean and sleek like a proud cat." JD stroked slowly up and down Fisher's back.

"I am not," he countered meekly, wanting to believe what JD told him.

"Yes, you are. Whoever filled your head with this 'you're not good enough' idea was full of it. You're smart, intense, caring...." Fisher opened his mouth to counter what JD was saying, but the words died on his lips when JD sat up, teasing around one of his nipples with his tongue. "See? Like a cat." Fisher arched his back, and JD sucked a little harder, sending zings of heat shooting through him. Within seconds, Fisher's pants were way too tight, his cock pushing at his zipper for release.

JD pressed him back, moving slowly, meeting Fisher's eyes. "Is this okay?"

Fisher nodded, and JD laid him back on the cushion.

"Dang," JD whispered and tugged at his belt. "You're something else."

"No, I'm just—"

JD put a finger to his lips. "Where I come from, when someone pays us a compliment, it's customary to say thank you. Not argue with them."

"You're playing the Southern card at a time like this?" Fisher asked, just managing to get the words out before groaning as JD popped the button on his jeans.

"Honey, I'm going to play all the cards I have." JD tugged at Fisher's jeans, and they parted. Fisher sighed in relief as his cock pressed forward in his briefs. JD tugged the fabric away and gripped him hard, stroking his shaft and grinning like he'd won first prize. "I wish you could see how you look right now."

"Me?"

"Yeah." He stroked again, and Fisher lifted his hips off the sofa, wanting more so badly his vision narrowed and all he saw was JD. "I could watch you like this forever. Your eyes are this deep blue, like the sky just before storm clouds roll in, and your cheeks are flushed and rosy. The best part is knowing that you're reacting like this for me."

"Yeah," Fisher breathed. "Okay...." He squirmed under JD's ministrations, wanting more, but not wanting this to end. He also wanted to see JD naked, but he couldn't seem to move his arms at the moment—or anything else. When JD shimmied back on the sofa, leaned forward, and then engulfed him in tight wet heat, it sent his mind skittering in a million directions, all of them leading back to JD.

Fisher whimpered and then groaned loudly as JD sucked him hard and fast. It was perfect, and he let JD know just how much he appreciated and adored that thing he did with his tongue that nearly blew Fisher's head off.

"Fisher," JD said.

It took a second for him to realize JD had stopped his trip to heaven. "Yeah," he gasped. "Please don't stop."

"I won't. But you do realize you have the filthiest mouth of anyone I have ever heard."

Fisher colored and blinked. "I didn't say anything."

JD brought his lips to Fisher's. "Honey, you let loose a string of profanity and dirty talk that would make a porn star gasp in openmouthed astonishment."

"I did?" Fisher asked.

"Yeah."

"I didn't know," he said meekly. "I'll stop it." Fisher clamped his lips together tightly, and JD sucked him deep. Within seconds he was once again on the road to delight, and JD seemed intent to get him there in the most mind-blowing way possible. "Not gonna last," he finally said, letting himself speak, and JD chuckled around his cock, sucking him all the way, holding still as Fisher quaked the entire time. "I want...." He trailed off, and JD pulled back. In a way Fisher was relieved, because he wanted to come and was not ready to come at the same time. It was too soon, but every brain cell he had screamed for release.

Fisher caught his breath and then pounced on JD. He actually leaped and sent him tumbling back on the sofa cushions. The couch groaned under the weight, but held together.

"You have so much energy," JD said through his chuckles.

"You're laughing."

"I'm happy that you're so delighted." JD kissed him hard enough to curl Fisher's toes. He never wanted it to stop; he loved being surrounded by JD's warmth and strength. He was safe for the moment, and that only added to his growing security.

Fisher stepped off the sofa, pants open, his cock jutting toward JD. He was a mess, and he loved it.

"You look debauched," JD told him.

"Not yet, but I'm getting there." He turned toward the back of the apartment. "Maybe we should go to the other room."

JD got up and took his hand, leading Fisher back toward his bedroom. "You have the dearest way of doing things sometimes."

Fisher tugged them to a stop. "Fooling around on the sofa is one thing, but going to the bedroom means...." He stopped because he wasn't sure what he was trying to say exactly. "This is my bedroom—it's where I sleep, and it's where I always feel safe when I need to." He turned to JD. "Do you understand?"

"I'd never hurt you," JD said.

Fisher shook his head and began tucking himself back into his pants. Instead of feeling sexy now, he felt exposed and bare in a way he hadn't expected. "I know that. At least I know you wouldn't on purpose. But I'm not talking about that." He huffed softly, afraid to say the words. "If you just want to fool around and have fun, then we can stay on the sofa, but if we go to the bedroom, then it means... something." What, he wasn't sure, but he knew he couldn't take JD in there if this was just some quick blowjob or a one-time fuck thing.

JD gave a quick tug, and Fisher ended up in his arms. "If you're asking for flowers and forever, I can't give you that, at least not right now. It's too soon. But if you're asking if you're my boyfriend, then the answer is yes. I want to get to know you and see what makes you tick. I love that you get all jittery when you're unsure about something, and then once you have the answer, you light up and brighten a room."

"I'm your boyfriend?" Fisher asked.

"Yes. If you want to be."

Fisher nodded and guided JD toward the bedroom and inside to his bed. Fisher loved his bedroom; it was bright, with warm, soothing colors. JD held him, and when Fisher wrapped his arms around JD's neck, he lifted him off his feet and set him on the bed.

JD caressed him, looking deeply into his eyes. For the time being the worries and cares that seemed to plague his mind all the time were silent. All that mattered was JD, who tugged off his pants and settled him back on the bed before stepping away to shuck his shoes and the rest of his own clothes.

What a sight—acres of warm skin covering thick corded muscles that seemed to dance with each movement. JD climbed on the bed and paused. "What's that look for?"

"You're the one who looks like a cat," Fisher said.

"No. I'm a bear, well, without all the fur. I'm too big to be a cat." JD straddled his legs, and Fisher wondered what was up. "I'm a big guy, but you're lean and smooth and wiry."

"Ugly," Fisher commented before he could stop it.

"No. Everyone wants to be what they're not. I'm big, but I like guys who are sleek and long." JD leaned closer. "You need to try to let go of your image of yourself." JD looked down, and Fisher followed his gaze to JD's jutting cock. "See what you do to me? That isn't fake or a figment of my imagination. You excite me."

Fisher swallowed. He wanted to believe what JD was saying more than anything in the world. "Really?"

"Honey, you're one hot number." Before Fisher could argue, JD kissed him, settling forward until their bodies pressed together. Fisher entwined his legs with JD's and let go. He reveled in skin on skin, sweat-slick and amazingly hot against his own. JD was careful and gentle, yet forceful enough to touch him in just the right way to make him quiver and shake. When JD slid down his body and sucked him hard and fast, Fisher arched his back. He lolled his head on the pillow and let JD take them both where he wanted to go.

"JD," Fisher whispered as he was about to crest the pinnacle of desire. "I can't…."

JD rubbed his belly, sucking him harder and deeper, stripping away the last of Fisher's control. He came in a rush that sent waves of pleasure crashing through his head. Through it all he felt JD shake, and then he held him. There was something to be said for feeling secure and safe, if only for a little while.

CHAPTER
Five

"PROCEED TO Bedford and Louther," Dispatch told him, and JD acknowledged the call, turned on his lights and siren, and hit the gas. Things seemed to be getting worse, not better. He'd answered three calls during his shift, and two of them were drug related. They had to find the source and shut it down.

JD pulled to a stop behind Red's cruiser and got out. A suspect lay on the ground.

"He isn't cooperating," Red said.

It seemed the young man had decided to go limp and not cooperate about getting into the cruiser.

"Maybe you should kick him in the gut? No one's around to see or care." JD winked and the suspect suddenly sat up.

"That's police brutality."

"No," JD corrected. "That's us getting you to do what we want." He chuckled and helped Red get the suspect into the backseat, then closed the door. "When I was at the station an hour ago, the mayor was in the chief's office again."

"I know. Did you see the paper? They as good as called our town a drug hub," Red said vehemently. "Where is all this shit coming from? We don't have that many users in town. So who's distributing it all? We apprehend people, but except for that guy who broke into Fisher's building, no one is talking."

"You'd think one of them would roll over."

Red shook his head. "Not a single one. They know if they keep quiet, it makes it harder for us to build a case, and this is way too much money for any of them to give up on. Someone is running a clearinghouse right under our noses, and we can't see them."

"What about the information he provided about them using trucks?" JD said.

"Too broad. Do you know how many trucks run on the turnpike every day?"

"So how did you get the last one?" JD asked.

"Almost pure luck. Terry and I stumbled on it almost by accident. No, these people are smart, and they're innovative. However they're doing it, it's right under our noses. I know it. The thing is, one of us may have even seen it and not known what was going on at the time." Red huffed. "I need to get him to the station for booking."

"My shift is almost over, and I need to face my mother. She messaged me that she's on her way from the airport." He looked longingly at the backseat of Red's car. "I'd rather spend the rest of the night patrolling the back alleys of town to root out every one of this guy's friends than face my mother for five minutes."

"That bad?" Red asked.

"If there's a firefight, be sure to call me. It would be less stressful." JD waited until Red was in the car and then followed him back to the station. Once he'd punched out, JD messaged Fisher, who called him right back.

"Do you want me to meet you at your house?" Fisher asked as soon as JD answered the call.

"You don't have to do this," he said for the millionth time. He really didn't want to subject Fisher to his mother. All he wanted was to find out what his mother had in her craw, put an end to her contesting Aunt Lillibeth's will, then get her out of town. "My mother can be too much for anyone." JD wished the sidewalk would open up and swallow him whole.

"I'll be there in ten minutes. I'm just getting my coat."

"Are you sure you're going to be all right?" Sometimes Fisher was so skittish, and others he was as carefree and brave as anyone else. JD knew it was part of Fisher's condition, and he needed to accept it and learn to assess how he was feeling. "Red told me today that we didn't catch the men doing the shooting yesterday. Officers are still looking and talking to neighbors. There was a blood trail, but it ended." JD hated bringing this up at all because he didn't want Fisher to freak out, but keeping things from him wasn't good either. "Those men most likely saw you. But it isn't likely they'd have the resources or the skills to track you down." He didn't want anything to happen to Fisher. "Just be careful and watch out around you."

"I have my phone with me, and you'll be there right after me." He sounded almost perky. It was wonderful, and JD wondered if spending the night together was the source of it. JD knew he'd woken with a smile, surrounded by Fisher's warmth. Granted, he'd had to leave early, and he'd hated walking out on Fisher while he was still asleep, but he hadn't wanted to wake him, so he'd watched him lying curled under the blankets for a few seconds before leaving Fisher to sleep.

"All right. I'll see you in a few minutes." JD hoped they beat his mother there. She'd said she was renting a car and would get directions. He hung up and got to his car, then drove as fast as he dared. He didn't see Fisher along the way, but as he parked, Fisher approached the car, peering in with a wide grin. JD hadn't realized how concerned he was until he saw him safe and sound.

"Someone's happy," JD said. Fisher blushed brightly as JD took his hand and they walked to the door together. "I like you like this. You have a great smile." JD let them in and closed the door. He turned to share a kiss with Fisher but heard a car pull up outside. He peered through the side window next to the door and groaned. His mother always did have perfect timing when it came to casting a pall over others' happiness.

"Is that your mother?" Fisher asked from behind him. "She does know she isn't on her way to the country club for tea, right?"

"That's my mother. The only time I see her dress down is for a garden party, and then it's a light dress... also by Chanel or some other designer." JD moved away from the window and took Fisher's hand, walking to the back of the house.

"But she's here."

"And I don't want her to think we were waiting for her." The bell sounded. "Go sit in the living room. I'll let her in." He was getting more nervous by the second and he hated it. He approached the front door and opened it.

"Jefferson Davis, are you going to leave me standing out here in the cold all day?"

He stepped back. "You might have brought a coat." He wasn't going to let her get to him, come hell or high water. She stepped inside and looked around, her nose getting a little bit higher. JD closed the door and motioned toward the living room.

"I'd like some hot tea," she said.

"I didn't know I was serving anything," JD said.

"I'm a guest in your house."

"One who invited herself. I just got home from work a few minutes ago." His mother stopped when she saw Fisher. "Mom, this is Fisher Moreland, my boyfriend. Fisher, this is Mary Lynn Burnside, my mother."

His mother stilled like a Greek statue at the Met, staring in utter disbelief. JD loved that he'd left his mother speechless. Maybe that would give him a chance in whatever game she was playing.

"Fisher. That's an interesting name," she said, holding her hands close to her body.

"Manners, Mother," JD ground out between his teeth and then scowled at her. "You are in my home." He'd heard the "under my roof speech" many times, and it was satisfying as all get-out to throw it back at her. Fisher had stood and was saying how nice it was to meet her as his mother finally extended her hand and let Fisher shake it. "Please have a seat."

"I can make some tea if you like," Fisher offered.

"Thank you," his mother said.

"The tea is in the cupboard next to the refrigerator, and the pot is on the counter." JD smiled, and Fisher seemed relieved to be able to get away.

"He has manners and at least knows when to leave a room," his mother said.

"Too bad you left yours in Charleston," JD countered and sat on the sofa across from her chair. "Why did you come, Mother? You want something, and it has nothing to do with Aunt Lillibeth's will."

"Lillibeth was your father's sister, and everything should have been left to him," she declared.

"Too bad you don't get to make those decisions. Aunt Lillibeth was very clear in her will what she thought of you and why she made the decisions she did. No court is going to give you the time of day. It seems Aunt Lillibeth anticipated your little fit of temper. So give it up and explain what you want."

"I was speaking with your father." Most likely *at* the poor man, but JD let it go. "It was wrong of me to call you and request that you not come to the funeral. That was selfish, and I should have thought more clearly about what your aunt would have wanted."

"Thank you," JD said, and he relaxed just a little. He was well aware that this could be his mother's way of softening him up. After all, the funeral was over. JD had indeed stayed away, to his regret, and his mother had ultimately gotten what she wanted. So an apology now, with just the two of them, cost her very little. "But I'll ask again. What is it you want?" The kettle whistled, and JD stood and went to help Fisher.

"How is it going?" Fisher whispered.

JD shrugged and got out some cookies. They were from the store but it was what he had. His mother would probably turn her nose up at them, but that was fine. At least he could offer something. He put them on a plate and carried it in behind Fisher with the tea tray.

The next few minutes were about pouring tea and getting settled once again. JD was pleased when Fisher sat next to him on the sofa. It seemed so normal and comfortable, even if his mother glared at both of them. Of course, for her, that was normal as well.

"So why the visit, Mother?"

She set down her cup. "Lately your father and I have…. Some of the investments he and I made a number of years ago haven't paid off." The color in her cheeks rose higher and higher.

"You and Dad are broke?" he asked, lifting the mug to his lips.

"We certainly are not, but things have been harder than they should be. We were anticipating that your aunt would leave your father…." She opened her purse and pulled out a handkerchief that she used to dab the corners of her eyes. "It's been dreadful these past few months."

"No, Mother," JD said firmly, answering her before she could ask the question. "I will not go against Aunt Lillibeth's wishes, nor will I give you what you want." He set his mug on the tray. "You go through money like it's water."

"Your father and I have worked hard—"

JD shook his head. "You've never worked a day in your life. You put on charity events, joined the right clubs, talked to the right people, and worried about the family image. And how things looked to people as shallow as you, never giving a thought to how much Dad made." JD stood. "You kicked me out months ago because...." He turned to face her. "Because I didn't live up to the expectations of your image of the perfect family or the perfect life."

"You turned your back on everything our family stands for and has worked toward for generations. We help a great deal of people because of our standing in the community." She stared daggers at Fisher, and JD took his hand.

"I was being the person I am. But you unwittingly did me a favor. I couldn't go back to you and Dad or fall back on our illustrious family name. I learned to budget and take care of myself. And you're going to have to do the same."

His mother paled. "Your father says that we'll need to sell some of our holdings...."

"Do what you need to do. I intend to be the custodian of what Aunt Lillibeth left me. I have no intention of throwing money down your irresponsible black hole." He let go of Fisher's hand and walked up to his mother, coming to a stop over her. "Mom, the clothes you have on your back cost more than I make in a month, and you're asking me for money."

"At least I didn't have an affair with the mayor's son," she screeched. "How embarrassing was that? Everyone in town said you seduced him, that you led him astray, and when—"

JD turned to Fisher. "Robert Jay and I started a relationship."

"He killed himself because of you," his mother said, breaking into tears. Again.

"Mrs. Burnside," Fisher said softly, but she was too far gone at the moment.

JD wasn't sure if it was real distress or part of an act. "It doesn't matter. Robert Jay and I were seeing one another, and word got out. His father went ballistic, and Bobby couldn't take disappointing his father and took pills. After that, the ire of anyone who mattered in town turned to me because, after all, I was the only one alive to take it. The mayor stepped down, and his wife disappeared from society."

"You left town and came here?" Fisher asked, and JD nodded. "I'm glad you did. Not that all the bad stuff happened, but I'm glad you came here and that I got to meet you. And you aren't responsible for Bobby or anyone but yourself." Fisher turned to JD's mother, eyes blazing with fury. "The only people to blame for anything are Bobby's parents, for turning their backs on him, and you, Mrs. Burnside, for not standing up for your son. If you want to place blame anywhere, look no further than the mirror." He stood, a bundle of fury that JD hadn't known Fisher was capable of. "Where is the unconditional love? That's what a parent is supposed to give. You're supposed to accept your son for who he is and stand up to the people on the outside. That's what family does, not turn on one of their own." His hands shook, and Fisher turned and stormed out of the room.

"Are you going to let him talk to me that way?"

JD tracked Fisher with his gaze and then turned back to his mother. "He's right, and this is my house, and he can talk to you any way he pleases." JD walked to the door. "Excuse me." He left and followed Fisher to the very back of the house, where he sat in the small family room that jutted out into the back garden. JD sat in the wicker chair next to Fisher's.

"I'm sorry," Fisher said, covering his face.

"It's all right. Hell, you were right, and what she said was too close to what happened to you, isn't it?"

"Different reasons, but the result was the same. Parents should treat their children better than that," Fisher said. "I know I get scattered and my emotions go all wonky, but I'm still their son."

JD ignored the drama he'd left in the other room, pulling Fisher into an embrace. "When you're right, you hit a bull's-eye." He rocked slowly back and forth, comforting Fisher as well as himself. "Family should be about more than what you do for them or how things look.

94

They should be the ones who love you for who you are. They should see the real you—faults and all—and love you anyway."

"I should go home and let you deal with your mother." Fisher didn't move, and JD continued holding him. "I wanted to be here for you, not make things worse."

"You didn't," JD's mother said from behind him. JD turned and held Fisher tighter as his mother stepped into the doorway. "I don't think things could have gotten much worse between my son and me."

"Go sit in the living room. I'll be in again in a few minutes," JD told her. All that really mattered at the moment was Fisher.

"Why are you smiling?" Fisher asked as he wiped his eyes.

"Because you standing up to my mother was a thing of beauty. You went at her with the tenacity of a bear. No one has stood up for me like that in a very long time. And you did it with the dragon lady herself. That took more guts than I've ever had in my life."

"No, it didn't. She isn't my mother, and I wasn't programmed from birth to do what she said and respect her. She's just someone who pushed one of my buttons."

"Standing up for me was nice."

"Wait till I open my big mouth at the wrong time," Fisher said, and JD rolled his eyes. "You should go see what she wants."

"I know what she wants," JD said.

Fisher shook his head. "She came here for something important, and it wasn't money. She could have asked what she did over the phone and gotten a no answer. I think there's something else, and it's harder for her to talk about."

JD squinted. "How do you know that?"

"I don't. It's just a feeling. If it's okay, I'm going to sit out here while you talk to her. If you need me, just let me know and I'll come in."

JD sighed. "I have nothing to say to my mother." He stood and crossed his arms over his chest. Fisher chuckled at him, and JD lowered his gaze, realizing he look like a petulant child. "All right. I'll go talk to her if it will make you happy."

"You only get one mother, and while it seems neither of us hit the Vegas jackpot, yours came all this way, so there might be some hope." Fisher pulled up the wicker ottoman and stretched out his long legs. An image of Fisher naked flashed through JD's mind, long legs stretched, JD sliding his hands up them toward.... He blinked and pulled his mind back to where it belonged. Before he could get sidetracked again, he returned to the living room. He sat down and waited for his mother to speak, nibbling on a cookie like he wasn't dying of curiosity.

"You really aren't going to help us?" she finally said.

"Mom, why should I mortgage my future to support your bad habits? You and Dad have plenty of assets. Stop buying designer everything. Cut back on what isn't important." He shifted to the edge of his seat. "Growing up, we always had everything. When Rachel wanted a horse, you got her one. I got a car at sixteen, and so did she. Yeah, Dad took me hunting each year, but that was all we ever did together. You and Dad were so busy that you bought us things and that was all."

"We did the best we could for you," she countered.

"Did you really, Mom?" JD pressed. "It took moving here for me to see things more clearly. I didn't have access to your money or credit cards. I live on what I make and nothing more. Believe me, that was a shock for a while. I don't go out to eat for every meal. My furniture is stuff that someone else has used, and I didn't have a designer do my home. But it's mine, and I worked for it." He sat back because he wasn't getting through; not that he had really expected to. "What is it you really came for?"

"Things haven't worked out the way I thought they would," she began, dabbing her eyes and then lowering her handkerchief. "I was wrong, okay?" she blurted. "Your friend was right. I blamed you for things that weren't your fault. I don't understand this whole gay thing, and I doubt I ever will. I spoke with the reverend after church last weekend, and he said that I needed to pray for your soul and ask the Lord to guide you back onto the right path."

"So that's why you're here? Out of fear for my soul? Because let me tell you that the all-knowing reverend talks a good game, but go stand outside that store just on the edge of town where they sell those videos and watch on a Friday night and see if you don't see someone familiar." JD held her gaze. "Yes, Mom. I was a police officer, remember? I saw people at their worst, and I said nothing when they attacked me." He loved that he was rocking his mother's world just a little. "Glass houses and stones, Mother."

"All right," she snapped and stood. "I don't know what I expected by coming here."

"You still haven't gotten to the point. Just say what you came to say."

She turned away. "Your father is leaving me," she said to the front windows. "He said that I'd driven our son away and spent us to the edge of bankruptcy." Her voice held something JD hadn't heard before: fear. His mother was never afraid of anything or anyone. "He's blaming me for everything. He moved out of the house a week ago, and I haven't seen him since. Rachel told me it was my own fault and then suggested we hold an auction to start selling things." She bowed her head, and her shoulders rocked up and down slowly. "I don't know what to do."

"So you thought you'd come here, ask for money, and then everything would be like it was before? You know this isn't going to work." He stood but didn't approach her. He was wary of showing her too much sympathy. "Do you love Dad? I mean really love him, like deep in your gut."

"I don't know. He's been my husband for thirty years. I...."

"Then I think that's the question you need to answer." JD was in completely uncharted territory. "Money isn't the answer to this problem. You and Dad have to figure out what you want and whether that includes each other anymore." His head was spinning at this unexpected development. Maybe after all these years his father had gotten tired of his mother doing the talking and having the damn opinions.

Fisher came into the room, and JD extended his hand. Fisher looked at his mother and then him before taking his hand briefly. They shared a quick smile, and then Fisher left the room once again.

"He's only after your money," his mother said.

"How would you know?" JD snapped. "And what a mean thing to say about anyone, especially coming from you. If anyone in this house is after my money, it's you. You're in my house, and I'm getting tired of this bitch act of yours." It was time to bring this to an end.

"Don't call me a bitch," she hissed, doing a marvelous impression of a snake.

He wasn't going to fall into that trap. "When you and Dad turned your backs on me, it hurt something awful. But that's nothing compared to what Fisher's family has done to him. So don't you dare cast aspersions on him! Fisher is a kind man with a big heart—something you'd know very little about. Maybe if you'd been warmer and less worried about the opinions of the pinheads in your charity groups, you'd recognize a quality, genuine person when you met one." JD's anger rose quickly, and his cheeks heated.

"JD," Fisher said softly from the doorway. "Your mother doesn't know anything about me. She can be suspicious if she wants. I would be if I were in her place."

JD and his mother gaped at him.

"Mrs. Burnside, I'm JD's boyfriend. I'm not interested in whatever money he may have coming to him." He came closer. "I got a call from work that they need some help and have asked if I can come in. I'm going to walk home and change." He turned to JD's mother. "It was nice to meet you." Fisher then got his coat and quietly left the house.

His mother seemed shaken. "Is he always like that?"

"How? Nice? Yes, he is. Fisher is a better person than either of us." He went to the window, watching as Fisher crossed the road and hurried down the sidewalk. "He puts others first most of the time, and he doesn't try to ram whatever he thinks down everyone's throat."

"He seems a little off to me," she said.

JD turned to glance at her. "Fisher is different, but he was smart enough to get your number in about two seconds and strong enough to put you in your place." He let the curtain fall back into place. "You know what?" he said. "I've had enough of this."

"What?"

"Fighting and sniping at each other. I'm your son, but I'm also a person and deserving of respect. You're my mother and deserve respect in return. So here's the deal. You can either treat me as such or go. I don't need you any longer. You cut me off, and now I think I'm going to do the same. Either you act civil and treat me with respect or there's the door. It's up to you. I'm not going to ask for your acceptance or come crawling back. Charleston is steeped in history. The place is proud of its past and all the things that took place there. Well, Charleston is history to me, and I'm not going back there. I have a life here."

"So you're going to sell what your aunt left you? That house has been in the family since before the War of Northern Aggression." He could hear her getting on her high horse. "I won't have it."

"Then you buy it." He grinned wickedly. "You seem to think you have a say. You don't. Maybe that's the problem." He let her sputter a minute. "I'm tired of fighting with you over something that's none of your business. You chucked me out, and now you want back in. The thing is, I'm not sure I want to let you." This was one of the hardest things he'd ever had to say, and he knew he was playing a dangerous game.

"You don't want to be part of your family?" she gasped.

"Not if the price of membership is you controlling everything. I like my life here, and I'm not going to leave it. I will conduct my affairs, business and otherwise, the way I want. My mistakes will be my own, and I can live with that." He was starting to understand the real purpose of this visit. His mother often rallied people around her cause, and that was what she'd hoped to do today. "How long were you planning to stay?"

"My flight home is tomorrow," she explained. JD had to give her credit. He'd been hard on her, but she was as straight and tall as always, holding herself high.

"Are you booked into a hotel?" JD asked as his phone rang. He snatched it out of his pocket, saw Fisher's number, and answered. "You okay?"

"No. There are people outside my building. They're hanging around, and I know one of them. He was the one with the gun from yesterday. He's wearing the same hoodie."

"Where are you?"

"In the Painted Unicorn, across the street," Fisher answered, his voice quivering.

"Stay there. I'll call it in and be there as soon as I can." JD hung up and made the call in to Dispatch, already grabbing his coat as he moved through the house. "Mom, I have to go. Fisher's in danger. Make yourself comfortable, and I'll be back as soon as I can." He didn't wait for a response. He was already out the door and jumping into his car.

He could have walked just as fast, but the car would provide protection. He pulled up to the Painted Unicorn gift shop as sirens sounded from multiple directions. He went into the shop and found Fisher in the back, sitting on a stool, a mug in his hand.

"It's okay. We'll be fine here," a white-haired lady said soothingly as she sat next to Fisher.

"What happened?"

"He stopped in here because he said he wanted to look around, but he was agitated, so I directed him back here," the lady said with a smile.

"The man who was shooting yesterday was coming out of my building. I went in here and called you." Fisher shook like a leaf. "What if he was inside my apartment?"

"Thank you," JD said to the lady. "I'm a Carlisle police officer, off duty at the moment, and Fisher is my boyfriend. He's been having some thug trouble lately."

"We all have, young man. These kids come in and think they own the place." She glared toward the front.

"Ma'am, I need to ask Fisher about what happened, but then I'd like to talk to you. Maybe all of this is related."

"You bet it is," she said. "Everyone is scared, and some people are even talking about closing up shop. These kids approach us and say that we're on their turf, whatever that means." She shook her head. Dang, she was feisty.

"I'm JD Burnside. I'll try to help." This had the potential to mess up the entire town. He turned to Fisher. "Tell me what you saw."

"It was the kid who was doing the shooting. He came out of my building, blue hoodie, said Michigan on it. The thing was, he had on orange and red sneakers. Ugliest things I've ever seen, and he was wearing them yesterday. I remember now. He also was wearing dark glasses," Fisher explained breathily.

"Okay. Stay here," JD instructed both of them. "I'm going out front to talk to the guys. "I'll be back as soon as I can."

"Okay. Ruth will take care of me," Fisher said.

The lady patted Fisher's hand and smiled. "Of course, sweetheart," she said as she refreshed their tea.

JD hurried out front and found Carter and Kip with a suspect. "He took off running when we arrived." He matched Fisher's description right down to the glasses.

"I think this is our shooter," JD said with a smile and received a sneer in return from the suspect. Kip got him in a car, and JD turned to Carter. "We need to check out Fisher's place. If he broke in, then we have more charges we can add." He also needed to know. If they had been inside Fisher's home, that would upset him even more.

"Did Fisher give a good description?" Carter asked.

"Yeah. Matches him to a tee. You'd think the idiot could change his clothes."

"We can't go on just clothes."

"The shoes are the big giveaway," JD said as they crossed the street. The lock to Fisher's building had been broken once again. Other units arrived, and they took a few minutes to explain what was going on.

"Try to get prints off the broken part of the mechanism—we might get lucky," Carter told one of the other units, and then they entered the building, climbing the stairs slowly. JD stayed back and let Carter take the lead.

"The apartment door is open," Carter said and called for reinforcements before slowly approaching. "It appears empty." He went inside, and JD stayed out until he heard Carter call that it was clear. The apartment seemed undisturbed except for the broken lock and door. That was a relief, but Fisher was going to have to call his landlord again. "They left things alone in here."

"Must have been specifically looking for Fisher," JD said.

"Don't know why," Carter said as he approached the door. "If they'd left well enough alone, they'd probably gotten off, but they pushed and now the guy's in custody."

JD thought for a few seconds. "I have an idea. Contact Detective Cloud and see if we can play the suspect who came after Fisher before off against this one."

"Wasn't he up for drugs?" Carter asked as they stepped outside.

"Yeah. And this guy was chasing after another guy with a gun. Likely drug related. We might get lucky and find out these two actually know each other. Wouldn't that be interesting?"

Carter nodded as he contemplated the idea. "It's worth a try."

"I'm going to get Fisher taken care of. Will you make sure the apartment is secured?" JD asked, and Carter agreed. JD strode across the street and found Fisher with Kip answering questions.

"I need to get to work," Fisher said nervously.

"All right, I think I have what I need for now," Kip said.

"I'll take you to work," JD said.

"You were going to talk to Ruth," Fisher reminded him.

"I'll talk to Mrs. Carmine," Kip said.

JD walked out to his car with Fisher and then followed his directions to his new workplace.

"You don't need to do this," Fisher said.

"Just call me when you're done, and I'll pick you up," JD told him. Things with Fisher were getting too close for comfort, and whatever was up, he intended to make sure Fisher remained safe. "They're going to have to fix your door and lock, so you may need to stay with me tonight."

"What about your mother?" Fisher asked, chewing his lower lip.

"I'll figure everything out. Try not to worry about it, and call me when you can." JD leaned toward Fisher, sharing a quick kiss, and then waited while he got out. Fisher raised his hand to say good-bye, and JD drove off. It seemed as though he'd been going in a million different directions today, and he still had to face his mother once again.

He drove home and went inside.

His mother was sitting on the sofa, reading a book, when he came in. "Is everything okay?" she asked.

"No." JD went through to the kitchen and pulled open the refrigerator door. He grabbed a beer, opened it, and carried it into the living room.

"Drinking already?"

"Don't start, Mother," he countered and flopped on the sofa. What the hell was he going to do next?

She set her book on the table without making a sound. There were times he swore she was a cat—well, maybe a panther. "You were always an active child. From the time you got up in the morning until you fell asleep, it was go, go, go. I see things haven't changed."

"And that's bad?" he pressed.

"I didn't say that. I was just commenting." She checked her watch. "Maybe you should make reservations for dinner."

"Where would you like to go? There's Chinese, a few diners, bars, Mexican, Italian, and Belgian. The last one is probably best, but I bet they're booked for tonight."

"Then what did you plan for dinner?" she asked as though he'd just spilled on her dress.

"Truth?" JD asked. "I expected to have kicked you out of the house, and then Fisher and I would have dinner either here or at his apartment. He's a really good cook, much better than I am, and he bakes bread too." His stomach rumbled at the thought.

"Sounds like he'll make a fine wife," she muttered.

JD slammed his hand on the table, the sound reverberating through the room like a shot. "We don't have those types of relationships. Not that there's anything wrong with being a wife and mother, but that wasn't how you meant it. You were being snide and derogatory, and I won't have it. Fisher is a good person and a fine man with more backbone than half of Charleston. Hell, he has more spine than Dad ever did. He stood up to you." JD was seconds from throwing her out. "I know you aren't stupid, so stop acting like it. This isn't one of your airheaded society gatherings where everyone in the room shares a single brain and takes turns using it. To answer your question, I'm going to make some dinner." He stormed out of the room and pulled open the freezer. He found a package of frozen meat ravioli and put some water on to boil, then got out some hamburger to brown and a jar of sauce.

"What are you doing in here?" his mother asked as she breezed into the kitchen.

"Making dinner."

"Please," his mother said as she moved him to the side, turned down the burner slightly, and then got out a smaller pan and proceeded to brown the meat, as well as putting his jarred sauce into a pan. She began sorting through the spices in his cupboard until she found what she wanted. "Your grandmother believed that women should know how to cook."

JD pulled up a stool and sat down. "I've never seen you in a kitchen except to tell the housekeeper what you wanted."

"It was what was expected," she said, shaking what he figured was oregano into the sauce before turning the hamburger and adding salt and garlic. "My friends didn't cook, and I wasn't going to disappear into the kitchen when I had the ladies over, so we had Magda."

"And now?" JD asked as gently as he could.

She paused in her stirring. "I don't know. I guess your father and I have a lot of talking to do."

"What about the whole him leaving thing?"

She shook her head. "Your father can threaten whatever he wants, but we've been through too much to give up now." She went back to her cooking. "Maybe I could make him dinner?"

"There's a lot to be said for a simpler life, without all the commitments, houses, dinners, and all that. You and Dad have spent a lot of years doing what you thought you had to. Isn't it time you did what you wanted and told everyone else to fuck off?"

"Jefferson Davis. I taught you better than that."

"The word *fuck* is what you object to? Really?" He opened the refrigerator and pulled out another beer bottle, opened it, and passed it over to his mother. "You're going to need this, because there are more words you're going to object to coming. When you hear one, take a swig. After a while you won't care."

"Don't be smart," she chastised but took a drink anyway. "You were saying?"

"Think about it. You turned your back on me because of what you thought others were going to think. Is that the kind of mother you really are?" He couldn't believe he was actually having this conversation with her. Frankly, he didn't think he'd get more than a few phone calls from her, and they'd involve a lot of yelling. "If it is, cool. The door is that way." He raised his eyebrow.

Her lips twitched. "You don't seem to be particularly broken up." She drained the meat and placed it in the sauce.

"Bobby and I cared about each other. Yes, he was the mayor's son. But he deserved to be loved and cared for the same as me, Fisher, or anyone else. Instead, his father dumped a load of hurt on him, and he took his own life. That wasn't my fault, as Fisher said. It was his father's, and there's a special place in hell reserved for him." He tapped the bottle of beer, and she picked it up. "I'm thinking the really bad part, where they flay you alive or something each and every day. At least that's what I hope happens to him."

"He's a good man," his mother countered.

"He wasn't to Bobby, and he can be as nice to everyone as he wants, but it isn't going to make up for driving his son to suicide." JD wasn't going to let this go.

She turned off the burners and sighed, staring at him. "Why didn't you do what Bobby did? Not that I wanted you to, but why?"

"Because I had Aunt Lillibeth," JD answered honestly. "She always told me to be who I was and not worry about what everyone felt, and she didn't turn her back on me when the rest of you did. Never would, no matter what." He leaned over the counter. "And I will have to live with the fact that I let you talk me out of coming to her funeral because of how my presence, which there is nothing wrong with, would have made you look." He hated his mother for that, and he hated himself for listening to her.

"That was wrong of me. People kept asking where you were."

"Let me guess. You made up some excuse rather than stepping up and telling them what you did," JD said, and he knew he was right when his mother didn't answer right away.

"I told them you were on a big, important case and that leaving would have jeopardized it." More lies to cover for the family. She mixed the pasta and placed it in a bowl.

JD stood and got two plates and set the table. "Don't you get tired of it? You lied about where I was, you lied about why I wasn't there. I'm sure you tell a dozen little social lies every day to cover for something. What kind of lies are you going to spin when the bills come due and you have to fess up that you can't pay them?" He got glasses and brought the food to the table. "It takes effort to lie and keep track of all of them. Just be done with it. I live an honest life."

"Yeah, I'm sure the men you work with know your little secret," she countered.

"What? Red is a fellow officer, and his partner is Terry. Carter has Donald, and Kip has Jos. The last two couples each have a little boy that they're raising together. They're good people. Just because they don't conform to your idea of what the ideal family is doesn't mean they aren't amazing people." He brought the beers to the table and waited for her. Once she sat down, he lifted his bottle and clinked it with hers. "This is about the last thing I ever expected in my life—to be sharing a meal with you again." In a way he was happy to spend some time with her, she was his mother, but this whole thing was weird, and he felt like he had to remain on the offensive in order to counter any attack that might be coming.

"I was raised to believe...." She trailed off.

"I know. Good old-fashioned Southern values," he grated out from memory.

"Family isn't outdated," she argued after taking a small bite. "This didn't turn out half-bad."

He nodded his agreement. "Family isn't outdated, but your view of it is." He set down his fork. "What if I were to tell you that I was going to adopt a child? Say, a little girl. Would you welcome her as your granddaughter or turn your back on her as well?"

JD had never seen his mother as rocked as she was in that moment. Conflict warred in her expression, and he could see the moment her jaw tightened. "Of course I wouldn't. A granddaughter. A sweet little girl. I've...."

"I know, Mom. You want grandchildren so bad you can taste it. How about a grandson for Dad to spoil and take hunting when he's older? Just because I'm gay doesn't mean I won't either adopt or have kids by a surrogate. It happens all the time. Would you turn your back on the next generation too?" JD began eating. There was only so far he could try to push his point before his mother dug in her heels and rejected everything he'd said. JD could tell that he was getting close by how set her jaw was and because if her posture got any more rigid, they could use her spine as a two-by-four.

He returned to his food to give her a chance to process what he'd said and for her rigidity to pass. Once she began to eat again, he remained quiet and left her to her own thoughts.

"How long have you known this young man of yours?" she asked.

"About a week, I guess," JD answered honestly.

"He seems a little… off to me," she repeated. "Not bad, just…. I can't put my finger on it."

"Fisher is a good person who's had a hard time of things for a few years." JD was careful not to betray any confidence. Fisher had told him what happened, but the story wasn't JD's to relate.

"I keep thinking of my cousin, Cora May."

"That's different. Cora May was born with a learning disability. Fisher was in an accident, and it threw off some of his body chemistry. But in both cases it wasn't their fault, and Fisher and Cora May had to deal with a world that wasn't kind to them a lot of the time."

"He seems nice enough," she said.

"Nice? Mom, he tore into you like a tiger."

She nodded. "But it was to protect you. That says a lot about a person and their feelings, even if they are less than tactful."

"You mean even if they are honest and it hurts," JD pressed.

"Why must you be so mean?" she asked, and JD stared back at her. That was the pot calling the kettle black. His mother could be the queen of mean, and often for no apparent reason other than to protect her image. "Fine. Let's not fight. I'm here only a short time."

"Fighting is what we do. It's how you and I have communicated for years. What else is there? If we didn't argue or go at each other, we'd never talk at all. It's rather pathetic but true." It had taken JD a long time to be able to let his mother's demanding and controlling nature roll off him, and then a great deal of pain before he'd fought back. "If you want something different back, then you need to put out something else."

"Are you telling me you get what you put out?"

"Yes, Mom." JD ate the last bite on his plate and took his dishes to the sink. He rinsed them and turned to his mother. "What, you think I'm a waiter?" He turned away again, and she brought her dishes over. "Think about what you've done and how people see you. That's how you're going to be treated. People who think you can do something for them are going to suck up to you, and others are going to go along so they don't make waves. That's how it was all through school. I was a Burnside, and I got what I wanted because of who you and Dad were. That isn't the case here. I have real friends who like me for me, not my money or influence. I'm not friends with the mayor, and it wouldn't matter if I were. The borough is run by a council. The mayor does very little. But I'm a police officer here, one of many. I'm respected and I earned that myself."

"So if your father and I asked you to come home...," she said tentatively. Something JD hadn't known his mother was capable of.

"This is home now. I've built a life here that I'm not going to walk away from." He finished the dishes and turned off the water. "No one cares what happened back home or about the mayor's son. They're good people who don't care if I'm gay or anything else. They accept me for who I am, and that's been what I've been looking for my entire life."

"If you aren't returning, who is looking after your aunt's estate?"

"Her lawyer is taking care of everything for me."

"You should transfer that to your father."

"No," JD said firmly. "Family and business do not mix. I won't mix the two." He wiped his hands on the dish towel and turned off the kitchen light.

"You know you can be a sanctimonious shit," she told him with a half smile.

"I had a good teacher." JD didn't give her an inch. "And yes, I suppose I can be. But I've been here six months, and I'm happier in Yankee land than I ever was at home."

She checked her watch. "I should go to my hotel and get checked in and settled."

"All right. I expect Fisher will be calling soon to have me pick him up."

"Doesn't he have his own car?"

"Someone broke into his apartment because he saw something." He didn't go into the details of the cocaine distribution happening in town. His mother didn't need to know, and after all he'd told her about liking it here, he didn't need to color that image. "I'll pick him up and make sure he's safe."

She got her purse, and JD walked her to the door. "I'll call you in the morning and we can have breakfast or something," she said.

"Mom, for me breakfast is at six."

She shivered but didn't say anything, just turned and walked out to her car. She got in the Lexus and pulled away from the curb.

JD went back inside and closed the door, then called Carter. "Did you find anything?"

"Well, we did what you suggested, and you were right. They knew each other, and they're connected, but they aren't talking. They simply clammed up and refused to talk."

"Do you know how they found Fisher?"

"They said they followed him, but I'm not buying it. Someone is pulling the strings. These guys aren't smart enough to follow and find him. Neither of them is going anywhere, but it's not going to do us a lot of good unless they're willing to make a deal. These guys are more afraid of the man behind the curtain than they are of us. Fisher's apartment was secured, and we called the property owner. He was less than pleased, but we explained that Fisher wasn't responsible for the damage and his anger drifted away. Take care of him. I have a feeling that there's more hurt waiting around the corner."

"Shit. That's all he needs. Fisher has been through way too much already."

"The best thing we can do is our jobs. Getting to the bottom of this will go a long way." Carter was right, of course. JD's phone beeped to indicate he had another call. He finished with Carter and answered the other. It was Fisher telling him he'd be ready in half an hour.

JD got ready and met Fisher at his workplace on time. "How did it go?" he asked after Fisher got in the car.

Fisher told him what they were doing, but of course it was pretty much gibberish to him. He'd never worked in a warehouse, but what was important was Fisher's excitement and enthusiasm. "We have to be ready for Monday, and we're getting there. I'll need to work Saturday and maybe even Sunday to get ready." JD parked the car in front of his house and took care of their coats before leading Fisher into the living room.

"I can make sure you get where you need to go," JD said, continuing their earlier conversation.

"I have a car. I can drive myself," Fisher said. "I'm not weak or helpless."

"I didn't think you were, but I'm just trying to make sure you're safe. We caught the suspect who was following you, but Carter says there's more behind it." He sighed. "I don't think you should stay alone right now."

Fisher fidgeted in his seat. "I'll call a hotel and see about staying there, then."

"Fisher, you can stay with me at the house for a few days," JD said. "It's fine."

"What about your mother?" Fisher asked.

"She went to a hotel, and she's going home tomorrow, empty-handed."

"Did you talk?" Fisher asked, and JD heard the longing in his voice. "She came all this way."

"I'm not sure we made much progress, but yes. She and I made dinner, such as it was, and we did some talking. I don't know if I got through to her, but we did talk. In our way. I'm more concerned about you. I have a guest room, and you're welcome to it if you want."

Fisher flashed a look that JD didn't understand. He wanted Fisher to sleep with him, but he wasn't going to press him or take advantage of a stressful situation. Fisher had had his apartment broken into, and JD knew that sort of thing left the victim feeling violated, because someone was in their personal space without permission. JD figured Fisher wasn't going to be up for anything physical and that he might need some time to himself to process what had happened.

"Why does this shit keep happening to me?" Fisher asked much louder than JD had expected. "I'm a quiet guy. I never get in anyone's way. I live my life and try to do the best I can, but I'm the guy everyone dumps on. I can't take all the shit that life seems to pile on me all the damn time." Fisher clenched his hands into fists. JD wondered if this pent-up anger was part of Fisher's condition, but he said nothing so as not to aggravate him further. "I'm just a guy who made some really bad mistakes, and now I'm paying for them time and time again." He began pacing the confined area like a caged dog. Fisher lifted his gaze from his feet, eyes shifting from side to side as if to try to remember if he'd actually said that out loud. "Dammit."

"What did you do?" JD asked suspiciously, the cop in him jumping to the fore. This was sounding more and more like the conversations they had in interrogation. Make the suspect angry to let their guard down, and things began to spill out.

"What most people with this disease do," Fisher explained a little more loudly. "I self-medicated after the accident. The bipolar highs are amazing. They make you feel like you can do anything. Want to run for president? Do it, because no one else but you can win. I wanted that feeling to last forever. It's an illusion, of course, but one I was ready to buy into. I'd take whatever I could to keep it going. Alcohol is crap, doesn't work, and brings on the low. I needed pills—uppers, things that make you invincible."

JD swallowed hard. "Like cocaine," he whispered.

"Yeah. I took it and it was golden. I was amazing. Everything I said was clever and insightful, and people wanted to be around me." He stopped moving. "It wasn't until I sobered up in a ditch that I got a clue how illusory the whole thing was. But it didn't fucking matter at the time. So I'd come down, and then I'd go chasing the dragon once again."

"You're not on that now?"

Fisher gaped and shook his head. "You've been around me. Do I look like I can afford or act like I'm taking cocaine? Hardest thing I ever did was ask for help to get out of the hole I'd dug, and it was halfway-to-China deep. But I did it and got on the right meds for my condition." Fisher sighed and slowly calmed down. "This is all that's left of that guy. This skinny, hollowed-out shell that feels everything through the filter of the damned medication." He turned away. "You don't need to be with someone like me. I'll never amount to anything other than a guy who checks in trucks at a warehouse. I don't even understand why you're being nice to me. I don't deserve it. I did some pretty bad things in order to get the drugs I wanted."

JD went cold, ice cold, and shivered in place for a few seconds. He was scared as hell to ask Fisher what it was he'd done. "How long ago?"

"When did I quit? A little over two years ago. That's when I got help, cleaned up, and got on the meds. But before that I ruined every relationship I'd ever had. The people at the shelter helped me sober up, and then they helped get me the apartment and worked with me so I could get a job and rebuild my life."

"And you don't think that was a worthwhile pursuit? That's hard as hell." JD still had images flashing through his mind of what Fisher might have done for his habit. He'd seen professional people, upstanding citizens, stoop as low as possible for their next fix. That high was all that mattered at the time. "And it takes a strong person to do what you did."

"Don't blow smoke up my ass and tell me we're having a good time. I let myself get that low. I was responsible for it. That was part of my recovery—taking responsibility for my actions."

JD did what he could to get his surprise under control. This was not at all what he'd anticipated talking about tonight. "Do you know the dealers and people around town?"

"I used to know them all," Fisher confessed, and his gaze went back to his feet. "I don't any longer. That was part of the therapy as well. Changing habits and not revisiting old haunts. If you want to make a change, then you do it with a clean break and don't look back. That's what I've tried to do, but that life seems hell-bent on pushing its way back, and you're a nice guy. You don't need to have me or anything else pull you into the gutter."

"Hey. You were strong enough to come back from the brink. I see people all the time that aren't. And you aren't going to pull me anywhere." JD crossed his arms across his chest in a show of strength to cover the quiver that raced through him. God, he had so many questions, but by looking into Fisher's eyes, he knew he wasn't going to get answers. They were locked tight, and JD had to decide if he was willing to take Fisher on faith. JD's insides growled at him. He was a police officer, and Fisher had just alluded to doing things that were illegal and had hinted at more that he didn't seem willing to talk about. "Fisher...."

"I can't talk about that," Fisher said, jabbing his hand toward JD's chest. "I can't. If I have to talk about it, then I have to relive it."

"And you don't remember...." JD filled in from the lost look that flashed across Fisher's face. "...everything that took place during those times."

Fisher nodded. "What I do remember is ugly, really ugly." He turned away. "Will you show me to the guest room? I think I need to lie down."

"Did you eat?" He turned toward the kitchen. There was pasta left from what he and his mother made. JD heated it up in the microwave and placed a plate in front of Fisher, who ate in silence, took his dishes to the sink, and thanked him. Then JD took Fisher upstairs, where he showed him the guest room and bathroom. "Good night," he said softly, closing the door before going downstairs.

He flopped on the sofa in the living room, turning on the television to some holiday movie that he ignored. What the hell was he going to do? He thought about running a background check on him. He was dating the guy and had called him his boyfriend, but what did he really know about him? He got frightened at shootings, but who didn't? JD still did. Fisher was nervous and cute in a gangly way. There were depths to him that he was only beginning to see. JD liked him. One of the guys at work could run the background for him; it didn't even need to be him actually doing it. The distance made him feel better in a way and dirty in another. Was he afraid of what he was going to find, and if he did run the background and Fisher found out about it, would he ever trust him again? If the tables were turned, would he want someone to run a background on him?

"JD," Fisher said from the living-room doorway. "Do you have a T-shirt or something I can borrow?"

He stood with a small groan and went upstairs to get some sweatpants and an old academy T-shirt from his drawers. He brought them to Fisher, who took them with a muttered thank-you and left the room. Fisher returned a few minutes later to the same doorway. "I told you I wasn't going to be any good to you. You deserve someone who isn't broken and useless." Fisher turned and climbed the stairs.

CHAPTER
Six

FISHER CLOSED the guest room door and sat on the edge of the bed. The room was sparse, with none of the warmth and charm of his own bedroom in his apartment, the one he wasn't sure he'd ever be able to sleep in again. What if he was lying in bed and someone broke in and tried to kill him? Fisher shivered, and that led to shaking, which in turn led to him nearly landing on his ass, racked with shudders that he knew started in his head but he couldn't stop. The shaking turned to all-out quaking as he tried to get to his feet and ended up on the floor once again.

In the end, he leaned with his back against the bed, holding his legs, trying to think of how he could possibly go home after all this. They'd tried busting into his apartment twice and had apparently succeeded the second time. JD had invited him to stay here so he'd be safe, but the truth was, he didn't feel it. Oh, he knew JD would never hurt him, and anyone would be foolish to break into a police officer's house. The entire force would come down on them like a hammer on the head of a nail. No, he wasn't emotionally safe. JD was way too close, and he thought that if he went downstairs and sat next to JD, he'd probably be held and comforted, something he wanted but was afraid to get used to. Everyone left or pushed him away, and it was best if this time he did the pushing. At least then he could walk away in one piece.

The resolve he'd had to talk to JD began to ebb. He could feel it flowing away just like his bipolar swings sometimes did.

"Fisher," JD said from outside the door, knocking softly. "I'm going to bed."

"Okay," he said quietly, hoping JD could hear him because he didn't have the energy to talk louder.

"You okay?" And there it was: concern, care. The things that were missing totally from his life, given without thought in only a few simple words. Fisher lowered his head to his knees, wondering how he was going to get through this latest crisis with his sanity and nerves intact.

"I don't know," he answered honestly and then wished he could suck the words back into his mouth. He closed his arms more tightly around his knees. The shitty thing was he didn't know what he was so upset about. He could pack his stuff and move again; he'd done it before. That was no big deal. It took him all of a few days. There wasn't all that much in his small apartment. The problem was how he was going to set foot in there again for any reason and feel safe. That was his happy place, the one location where the world stayed outside and couldn't reach him. Now that was gone. His home had been invaded by not just the men who had broken in, but by his old life, the one he'd done his best to try to keep at bay.

The knob turned, the gleam from the light changing slightly as it moved, and then the door opened. JD stood in the doorway. "What are you doing down there?" He hurried over and placed his hand under Fisher's arm to help him up. "A panic attack?"

"Yeah," he said quaveringly and once again sat on the side of the bed.

"I hate the word victim," JD said. "It makes the person on the receiving end of a crime seem like they have no recourse and are at the mercy of the criminals. Some people are victims. They let the criminals win, roll over, and try to deal with what happened to them. Others take it in stride and go on with their lives as a way of flipping a big fat bird." JD flipped his middle finger at the doorway. Fisher couldn't help laughing. It was funny seeing JD act this way.

"Okay," Fisher said, doing what JD did and flipping the bird. "My only question is what did that door do to you to make you want to flip it off? The poor thing just opens and closes. Maybe it whapped you on the butt once."

JD waited a few seconds, and then he laughed and sat down on the bed next to him. "A sense of humor does a lot. You know that."

"Yeah, but it doesn't mean I can go home and stay in the rooms they were in. It's creepy. What if they went through my stuff?"

"From what I saw, they didn't get far, and most things looked undisturbed. Carter and I were there pretty quickly, and they got the hell out of there. They seemed to be looking for you." JD took his hand. "Were either of those men your suppliers from before?" He probably had to ask, but it made Fisher's stomach turn over.

"No. But they could be working for one of the men who supplied me. He wanted to move up to bigger and better things. But I haven't seen him since I told him not to come around me anymore. That was a few years ago. His name was Zeus or something like that. I know it was a fake name, but that's how I knew him. We did our business, and then I stayed away when I wanted to get clean. I promised I'd never mention him if he'd turn his back and leave me alone. He did, and I'd forgotten about him until now because I wanted something I couldn't get from a snort. But now I know that I don't deserve what I wanted. It's not for people like me."

"What?" JD asked.

Fisher closed the gap between them. "I'll only taint anyone I care for."

"I don't believe that. If you want to change your life, then you can't be afraid to open your heart." JD moved a little closer. "We all get hurt. Goodness, my mother was here, and we sniped at each other the whole time, but I still love her. Even after what she did. When she got out of her car, I wanted to hate her, but I didn't and don't."

"That's easy to say, but it's harder to do when the reminders of everything that's left you behind or what you want to leave in the past keeps showing up like a bad dollar."

"You mean penny," JD corrected.

"Nah. No one deals with pennies anymore."

"You're a smartass sometimes," JD told him. "See what I mean about that sense of humor? You dig into it whenever you get really nervous or upset. It's a good thing to do."

Fisher leaned against JD and closed his eyes. "Sometimes I get so tired of trying to hold everything together. People look at me and expect me to go crazy, so I have to always be on my guard and not seem…

carefree or energetic, because then people wonder if I'm going to lose it or something."

"You just need to be yourself for me." JD put an arm around his shoulder, holding him a little closer, leaning right back. Then Fisher felt him turn and followed suit, letting JD kiss him. But the touch and taste of JD left him wanting more. He changed positions, sliding his arms around JD's neck, deepening the kiss. This was heaven, with all his attention and focus pinpointed on JD. The whole apartment thing fell away and so did his worries about not being good enough. JD had a way of making him feel special, and he did it with a single kiss. That was all it took.

"Do you want to stay in here?" JD asked.

Fisher didn't answer right away. It would be best if he slept in here, separate from JD, but his body most definitely had other ideas, and without thinking too deeply, he went with his instinct and allowed JD to tug him to his feet and kiss him out of the room and down the hall.

They didn't part as JD opened his bedroom door, propelling them toward the bed. Shoes were kicked off and shirts got tugged over each other's heads. Fisher didn't waste a second before pressing his hands to JD's strong, full chest. JD was virile, and he wanted him. That was almost more than Fisher could believe, but the physical evidence was too large and prominent to ignore. JD hitched his hands in the waistband of Fisher's shorts, tugging them to the floor. When Fisher stepped out of them, naked, his self-consciousness came roaring back, but JD hugged him close, rubbing down Fisher's back, cupping his ass in large, strong hands, and then Fisher was off and running.

"Is this good?" JD murmured against his lips.

Fisher closed the gap, kissing him harder, wishing for a lot fewer clothes on JD, but not wanting to put any distance between them to actually get them off. Fisher nodded—or maybe he thought he nodded, he wasn't sure. In his mind he was screaming the word, but his lips were otherwise engaged.

"Why ask that now?" he finally asked.

JD stilled, and Fisher nearly dove into the depths of his eyes. "I want this to be good, special."

"It is." Fisher groaned and wriggled a little as JD stroked his backside.

"Is it better than the high you used to strive for?" JD asked.

Fisher cupped his cheeks, holding their gazes locked together. "This is so much better than that, because it's real. The highs before were all illusion. There was no basis. The euphoria was all in my mind. In reality, it was ugly and a mess. So this doesn't compare to that at all." Fisher closed his lips over JD's, exploring his mouth as excitement made his ears ring. "Now take me to bed and make love to me." He used those words very deliberately, and he knew the moment their meaning kicked in.

JD lifted him and set Fisher back on the bed. He lay naked, no clothing, exposed to JD's gaze but surrounded by warmth and acceptance. What could have made him vulnerable only heightened his desire as he feasted on the sight that was JD. He wanted to hoot and holler, but settled for a brief whistle when JD bent over to take off his pants. The backside on him was a sight to behold, a natural thing of beauty.

When JD turned to face him, Fisher let go of the last of his reserve, quivering as JD gripped each ankle and slowly ascended. His legs shook by the time JD got to his thighs, and his eyes were probably as wide as saucers when JD slid his hands to his hips and then up his chest. Fisher spread his legs, and JD moved right between them, nestling his legs in between Fisher's and then lowering his chest to Fisher's.

"No one ever made me feel like you do," Fisher whispered. "No one and nothing."

"That's good to know." JD grinned.

"I want you," Fisher whimpered, encircling his legs around JD's waist to punctuate exactly what he was asking for.

"Okay. What do you like?" JD asked. "I know that sounds dumb at a time like this, but I want to make this special, and...."

"I want you, hard, full-on, and as deep as possible."

And that was exactly what JD gave him. By the time JD was done with his lips and hands, Fisher had been reduced to incoherent mumbles and groans while he clutched at the bedding to keep from flying apart. When JD entered him, slowly, at a glacial pace, his entire being cried out for more, but JD seemed determined to drag out what Fisher wanted for as long as possible.

"Guys like it fast," JD said. "So the best way I've found to heighten the fun is to go slow, draw things out."

"You're evil," Fisher said, rolling his head back and forth on the pillow when JD, his condom-coated cock buried inside him, didn't the fuck move.

"I'm going to make you feel good." JD still didn't move, but he did trail his fingers over Fisher's chest, circling the nipples in an exercise in teasing that had Fisher growling roughly.

"Then move, dammit." He pulled JD down, kissing him hard, and JD finally thrust his hips. There was only so much he or any guy could take. Fisher arched his back, groaning for more, pleas that JD ignored. "You are a stubborn ass sometimes."

"Yes, but you love it." He punctuated his words with rolls of his hips.

JD's cock slid over that spot inside him, and Fisher's vision blurred and his eyes crossed. God, he wanted this all day, every day. How had he managed to live all these years without this sense of fullness or rightness? The jumbled thoughts that always seemed to race willy-nilly in his head lined up and settled.

"Better?"

"God, yes," Fisher breathed and tightened his hold on JD's shoulders, meeting each thrust of JD's hips.

JD was gorgeous, glistening with sweat, chest pumping, belly rippling, eyes glistening as he looked at Fisher. There was no place he'd rather be than basking in the glow that was JD. "I'm not going to let you go."

It was too much for Fisher to believe that JD knew what he was saying or meant those words the way Fisher so desperately wanted to take them. Having someone he could rely on, to be there always, was more than Fisher's experience would allow him to believe. Regardless, hope sprang from a long-lost well inside, and Fisher grabbed for it. "Don't want you to," he finally managed to say. He wanted to stay like this forever, riding the wave of endorphins with JD to guide the surfboard. He never wanted this to end, but as the waves grew greater, his ability to control them lessened, and soon Fisher was on the edge. It looked to him like JD was there as well. His strokes became faster, deeper, stronger, and more frantic. Fisher closed his eyes, not wanting to miss the sight of JD coming, but afraid the pressure would become too much.

Fisher nearly flew to pieces with ecstasy as his release broke over him. "Jay... Dee...," Fisher cried and held on tight. The afterglow was more intense than any chemical high he'd ever experienced, and JD was right there with him, grounding him but still letting him fly. When he slowly returned to reality, Fisher opened his eyes to JD's smile. "That was amazing."

"Yeah," JD agreed. They shook as their bodies separated, and JD got up, threw out the condom, and returned with a warm cloth. Fisher reached for it, but JD gently pushed his hand aside, washing Fisher with small, gentle strokes and then drying his skin.

Fisher listened as JD moved around the room, taking care of the cloth and towel, putting out the lights. The bed dipped and JD pulled down the covers, then lay down right next to him. It took a few seconds for both of them to find a comfortable position, but Fisher ended up in JD's arms with his head resting on JD's chest, his heart beating a steady metronome of strength in Fisher's ear.

"Do you have everything you need for now?"

Fisher nodded.

"Then after work tomorrow, I'll take you to your apartment, and we can get everything straightened out," JD told him, and Fisher hummed his agreement, his eyes too heavy to remain open.

A DOOR closed some distance away, but it was enough to cut through Fisher's dream. He blinked a few times, remembering where he was and that the warmth that surrounded him came from the man sleeping soundly next to him. He stilled, wondering if he was hearing things, but a scrape made him rock JD's shoulder. "There's someone in the house," Fisher said.

"Jefferson Davis." A female voice with a Southern accent drifted through the door.

"God, it's my mother," JD said.

"What time is it?" Fisher asked, relaxing for a second when he realized someone hadn't broken in, but nervous about JD's mother being in the house.

"Five," JD answered, sitting up. "She said she wanted to have breakfast, and I told her breakfast for me was at six, so.... Wait. How did she get in the house?" He threw back the covers and sat on the edge of the bed. "Stay here if you like. I'll find out what's going on." He pulled a robe from the closet and left the room.

Fisher figured he might as well get up. He was needed at work in a few hours, and knowing that JD's mother was downstairs was a surefire way to ensure he didn't go back to sleep. He located the shorts he'd been wearing on the floor and pulled them on. Once he was dressed, he left the room and stopped to look in the guest room, where the shirt and sweatpants JD had loaned him sat folded at the bottom of the bed.

Voices drifted up the staircase, and Fisher followed them.

"Mom, how did you get in?" JD asked as Fisher reached the bottom of the stairs.

"If you didn't want me to come in, you shouldn't have put the spare key under the flowerpot, just like we do at home. And I wanted to do something nice for you," Fisher heard JD's mother say as he followed the voices through to the kitchen.

"Morning," JD said, greeting Fisher with a kiss much deeper than was necessary. Not that Fisher was complaining, but he couldn't help wondering how much of it was for effect. "I'm going to go up and get dressed. I won't be gone long."

Fisher's gaze shifted to JD's mother, and then he nodded.

JD left him with Mary Lynn, and he pulled out a chair and sat at the table, watching her try not to look at him. It was nice to know that she was as nervous as he was.

"So, Fisher…."

"Yes," he prompted. "Go ahead and ask what you want."

"It's obvious you stayed last night," she observed.

Fisher curled his lips upward as warmth spread through him at the mere allusion to what they'd done last night. "JD is a very special man." To Fisher's surprise, Mary Lynn poured a cup of coffee and brought it to him.

"He's my son," she said, as though that accounted for everything about JD. He didn't know what to say without being rude, and she made him nervous enough as it was, so Fisher sipped the coffee and kept quiet. "Do you and he…?"

"I don't think that's any of your business," Fisher said.

She turned around, looking like she hadn't slept a wink all night. "I'm trying to understand all this… gay stuff." She whispered the last two words.

"If you say the word gay, you suddenly aren't going to find yourself attracted to women. And you didn't do anything to make JD gay." Fisher figured that might be what she wanted to hear. "He was born that way."

"But why can't he just put that aside and be like everyone else?" she asked, setting the knife she was using to cut bagels on the counter.

"Why can't you decide tomorrow that you want to get divorced and marry another woman?" Fisher countered. "Because that isn't who you are, and why should JD spend his entire life being miserable being with a woman? Furthermore, what kind of life do you think she'd have? Being gay is largely about the gender of the person you fall in love with. Doesn't JD deserve to fall in love and be loved?"

Mary Lynn didn't answer right away. "But what if he hasn't met the right girl yet?"

"I could ask you the same question. Maybe tonight we could take you out to the bars and help you find the woman of your dreams." Fisher watched over his mug as Mary Lynn did the best imitation of a fish. "You want him to be straight for your own comfort. But that's bullshit. JD is the man he is, and you need to accept that and him, because JD is amazing."

"He is?" she asked, sounding surprised.

"Ye-ah," he said, exaggerating the word. "If you spent more time with him, you'd know that." Fisher couldn't understand how she didn't know that. "How much time have you spent with him?"

Mary Lynn turned away and went back to carefully cutting the bagels.

"That much." He sipped again from his mug and watched as Mary Lynn fumbled the knife. She huffed and slapped it down onto the cutting board.

"I know my son," she snapped, and a surge of nervous energy raced through Fisher. He did his best to tamp it down. "He's…."

"No, you don't. I'm guessing you saw him the way you wanted to see him." Fisher stood. "But, Mary Lynn, the real JD is so much better than that. You need to get to know him. The real him."

She banged two halves of a bagel into the toaster, and Fisher wondered what the appliance had ever done to her. Tension rolled through the room, and Fisher thought Mary Lynn was going to explode at any second. "What do you know about my son?" she challenged.

"JD can see what's inside people," he finally answered after giving it some thought. "He also sees what others don't. To most people I might as well be invisible. I go to my job, where I sit by myself in a booth most of the day, and then home to my small apartment. I spend a lot of my free time sitting on the bench in the square, watching people as they go by. I swear no one would have paid any attention, short of me hopping on the bench to do a striptease. But JD saw me, and he's tried to understand."

"What's to understand?" Mary Lynn asked.

Fisher hesitated to answer just long enough for strong fingers to rest warmly on his shoulders.

"Nothing you need to worry about," JD answered for him and then inhaled. "Cinnamon raisin, my favorite." JD got plates and put the fixings on the table. When the last bagel popped up, he brought that over with the rest of them too. "What time is your flight home?"

"I changed it last night. I leave tomorrow at noon." Fisher felt her stare. "I think it's time you and I tried to get to know one another. So I can spare one more day."

"What are you going to do while I'm at work?" JD asked, shaking his head slightly as he rolled his eyes, shoulders slumping. That clearly wasn't what JD had been expecting.

"I'll poke around a little. I most certainly can occupy myself for a few hours. Maybe we can do something fun when you're done."

Fisher wondered what Mary Lynn's definition of fun was. "You were going to help me with my apartment," Fisher reminded JD softly. "But I can take care of things so you can be with your mom." That was more important. He would figure things out.

JD finished spreading cream cheese on his bagel and took a bite. "Don't worry. I'll stop by to make sure a door has been installed, and then when you get off work, we'll make sure the apartment is secure."

As JD finished his breakfast, Fisher ate half a bagel. Then JD insisted on taking him to his apartment to change and then on to work. At first he protested, but JD said he wanted to keep him safe, so Fisher had backed down. It ended up worth it just for the kiss that JD planted on him. "Call me when you're done. They owe me some hours, so I'm going to try to take them this afternoon."

"It's good for you to spend time with your mom. It'll help heal what's between you," Fisher said.

"I'm not so sure."

"JD, she's here, isn't she?" Fisher asked and then stepped back. "All right. I'll call you when I'm done."

FISHER WORKED like a dog, but they made amazing progress. The systems and locations were set up a little after noon, and for the rest of the weekend the systems guys would test it, but it looked like they would be ready to start receiving on Monday. Ellen thanked him for coming in to help and told him he could have Sunday and Monday off.

"JD," Fisher said when his call connected. "I'm done here."

"Good. I'll be done in half an hour."

"I can wait," Fisher said and sat in one of the chairs in the lobby. Soon enough JD pulled in, with his mother in the passenger seat. Fisher got in back and pulled the door closed. "Are we doing something special?"

"Jefferson Davis was telling me about the antique stores you have here. He said things were different from what we have back home, so I asked him to take me. Jefferson Davis said that you'd probably like to go too."

She turned back around, and Fisher saw JD mouth, "I'm sorry," in the mirror before pulling out.

"There's the really nice one downtown," Fisher said. "But they're only open weekdays."

"How can they make a living like that?" Mary Lynn asked.

"They do a lot of their business on the Internet," Fisher explained. "There is one out west of town that I haven't been to in a while."

"Good. We'll stop there on our way back." JD continued through town and pulled into the parking lot of one of the stores they'd visited together. JD waited for his mother and fell in step with Fisher. "I know we've been here, but I was thinking we could make out in the back while my mother looks around." His wicked gleam told Fisher he was only half kidding.

124

"Boys," Mary Lynn said indulgently as she went inside. "Behave." There was little sting in her words as she disappeared inside. JD held the door, and they stepped into the dusty, musty space. The first thing Fisher did was look behind the counter; he was relieved to see that his ex's boyfriend wasn't there.

They spent the next ten minutes meandering behind Mary Lynn as she browsed. "I'm going to use the restroom," JD said. Mary Lynn had wandered into one of the booths, and Fisher wasn't sure if she wanted company or not. He hung back, letting his gaze drift for a bit. The merchandise was the same he'd seen before and held little interest. He checked on Mary Lynn, who seemed content to browse. The bell on the front door rang, and Fisher glanced at the incoming customer.

Instantly he tensed and backed into the first booth he could find. He knew the man from his past, and it was someone he never wanted to see again.

"I was here yesterday and called to have the wooden box set aside." That voice sent a chill through him. Fisher peered around the corner. Armand's back was to him, and Fisher took that moment to walk deeper into the store, away from the desk. He rounded a corner in the back and ran right into JD.

"Hey," JD said lightly, and his smile faded. "What is it?"

"The man at the desk. I know him from before… from what we talked about last night." Damn, he had to get this shaking under control.

"What was he doing?" JD asked, snapping to alertness.

"Picking up an item he'd called about," Fisher whispered. "He'll know me if he sees me."

"Is he a dealer?" JD asked, and Fisher nodded. "Get my mother and take her to the restroom." That had to be the weirdest thing Fisher could imagine JD ever saying. "Tell her it's for her safety."

"What are you going to do?" Fisher asked, but JD pointed, and he found Mary Lynn two booths over.

"JD says I need to take you to the restroom. There's something going on," Fisher explained and motioned her toward the back of the store. It was a single-person restroom, but they both stepped inside, and Fisher locked the door.

"What's all this about?"

Fisher contemplated his answer and figured playing dumb was probably best, so he shrugged and turned away. The bathroom was ancient, with stained fixtures and discolored paint. The floor was cracked, and the toilet seemed to run constantly. "He said to tell you that this was for your safety."

She nodded and stood in the center of the space, arms pulled in, probably so she didn't touch anything. Not that Fisher could blame her. "How long should we wait?"

There was a soft knock on the door, then "It's JD." Fisher unlocked it and stepped out. JD put a finger to his lips. "It's time to go. Talk normally. We're getting out of here." JD took his mother's arm. "Did you find anything?" he said in as normal a tone as possible.

"Not this time," Fisher answered.

"But you never know," Mary Lynn added as they approached the front door. "Thank you," she said to the man behind the counter, and they left the store and got into JD's car. "What was that about?" Mary Lynn asked as soon as the car door closed.

"Fisher saw a guy he recognized as bad news." JD turned to Fisher. "I only saw his back as he was leaving. I did get a license plate, but he wasn't doing anything illegal...."

"Nope. Though I wouldn't have pegged Armand as the kind of guy who collects antiques."

"What did he get?"

"A wooden box. I got a glimpse of it, and I don't know why anyone would bother with it. There was nothing special other than it was an old wooden box." Fisher waited to see if JD could enlighten him, but he started the engine and drove back toward town. "What are you thinking?"

"I'm not sure. I wish I could have gotten a closer look at what they were doing."

"I'm just glad he didn't see me," Fisher said.

"Are you involved with drugs?" Mary Lynn asked. "I saw this on television once, or was it one of those awful movies your father likes? The suppliers use the businesses, and they pass the merchandise to the dealers inside regular purchases."

"Isn't that a little far-fetched?" JD asked.

"Why would it be?" Fisher leaned forward in the backseat. "Remember the last time we were here? A guy came in to pick up an item he'd called about. That ugly vase. What if it was filled with drugs, the same with the box? Armand is no Boy Scout, and he doesn't collect old boxes. He collects customers and money." Fisher was beginning to warm to this theme. "Think about it—who would pay attention to the activity around an antique store? People come and go all the time. They have regular customers. And lots of cheap things they can put the real merchandise in."

"It seems...." JD pulled up to the main intersection on the square and into a parking space. "I need to make a call." He got out, and Fisher sat back, waiting for JD to return. Neither he nor Mary Lynn made conversation, and after a few minutes JD returned and they pulled back into traffic, going west, out of town.

Fisher and Mary Lynn wandered through the second antique store while JD stayed outside on the phone. "Has JD always been that intense?" Fisher asked.

"Goodness yes. He threw his whole self into everything he did. And he was always determined to be the best. If he played baseball, he had to have the most home runs. When we signed him up for tennis lessons, he had to beat everyone right away." She looked around. "This store is much nicer than the last one."

"Yes, it has a lot of interesting things." Fisher kept an eye out for JD, hoping he'd join them soon. The purpose of this little outing was for JD and his mother to be able to talk. "Do you collect antiques?"

"The house is full of family pieces that were collected over time. Mostly no one threw anything out, ever, so what we had got old and desirable again."

"I have some family pieces too," Fisher said. "I've also gotten a few on my own." He turned to Mary Lynn. "What I'd really like to be able to do is to make my living selling antiques. I've read all kinds of books, and I've spent a lot of time at auctions and things, so I know what things are, how to research, and then how to arrive at a value. Half the time it's just being able to tell the real thing from a fake." He'd forgotten who he was with and grew quiet. JD's mother made her way up and down each and every aisle, looking into each case, but not saying anything. It was a little unnerving. "I know this isn't what you're used to."

She scoffed slightly. "Do you know how rich people stay rich?"

"By having a lot of money and not spending it," Fisher said.

Mary Lynn shook her head. "You have to spend money like a rich person." She walked over to a case and pointed to a small painting in the back. "Let's say that's a Van Gogh or some other famous artist, and I buy that for a million dollars. I hang it on my wall and enjoy it for a few years. Then I turn around and sell it for two million because the artist is famous and not painting anything more. I've been able to enjoy the picture and so have my friends, it goes to a new home, and I get paid a million for the pleasure. That's how rich people spend money and stay rich. They buy things that will hold their value and even increase. That goes for real estate, art, furnishings, vacation homes, all of it. The prices of those luxury goods keep going up."

"I see."

She stepped closer. "No, you don't. Because that goes for you too. Buy the best quality you can afford, because later you can sell it and buy something else. It's what the antique dealer in you will capitalize on." Then to Fisher's surprise, she smiled, a genuine, warm smile. "It's the biggest untold secret of wealth ever. Since we all have to buy things, make what you buy count."

He wanted to ask about the clothes she was wearing, which looked expensive, to see if that fit into the equation as well.

"I see you thinking," she prompted and looked down at her outfit. "I'll let you in on a secret. Quality clothes will last you a long time too. This is Chanel, and I've had it for years. Every now and then, I pull it out and it seems new again. Oh, I have my weaknesses, mainly shoes and handbags, but it works with them as well. Quality never really goes out of style—it just takes a vacation every now and then." She began working her way back toward the front. "Jefferson Davis, I thought you'd left us here," she scolded lightly when they encountered JD.

"We should go home," he said seriously before turning toward the door. He strode out, leaving Fisher to walk with JD's mother.

"I thought I raised him better than this," Mary Lynn said.

"That's the cop in him," Fisher explained. "He gets really serious and closemouthed when he's working through something important and can't talk about it."

"How do you know?" Mary Lynn asked, bumping her shoulder against his almost conspiratorially. "I mean, you haven't known him all that long."

"It's his eyes." Fisher stopped right there. He wasn't going to tell JD's mother that he got that same intense, fiery look in bed as well. That was private. "He'll tell us once we're out of here." He reached the door, saying good-bye to the man as they walked in front of the desk.

"Let's get in the car," JD said, hustling them inside and then pulling out. "We need to go back to the station. Red and Detective Cloud want to talk to you."

"Me?" Fisher asked.

"Yeah. Mom, I can take you to your hotel."

"No, thank you. I'm going along," she said firmly. "Nothing fun like this ever happens at home." Fisher had to admit that once Mary Lynn pulled the stick out of her rear end, she was an interesting lady.

"Mother."

"Don't 'Mother' me. You were in an all-fired hurry to get us out of there, so you need to get Fisher where he needs to go, and I'm going to go with him." She sounded tickled pink, while Fisher was instantly on the verge of a panic attack. He didn't like the sound of police questioning. What if he said something he shouldn't? Or if they asked him questions and then wanted to know how he knew something? Scenario after scenario ran through his head. At one point, he thought about jumping out of the car and going right home.

By the time they pulled up to the station, Fisher was consumed with worry and nearly catatonic. He got out of the car without thinking and followed JD inside, but he had totally pulled inside himself.

"It's going to be okay. Red and I will be there," JD said.

"Yeah, okay," he answered half consciously. He knew "Detective Cloud" meant that man who had questioned him at the scene of the shooting and he wasn't interested in spending any time with him.

"We're going to go in here," JD said and opened the door to a conference room. Fisher sat down at one of the seats, with Mary Lynn on one side and JD on the other.

"I'm Detective Cloud."

"I remember you," Fisher said, looking down at the table.

"Let me," Red said. "Fisher, we're interested in knowing about the man you saw in the store this afternoon."

"Armand," he answered. "He was and probably still is a dealer." He lifted his gaze slightly. "He didn't see me, thank goodness."

"He'd know you?" Detective Cloud asked. "How would he do that?"

Fisher looked to either side. "He came into the store and said that he was there to pick up a box that had been held for him. The guy behind the counter gave it to him, and by the time I could find JD, he'd apparently left."

"Did you hear the cash register?" Red asked.

Fisher searched his memory. "No. I don't remember hearing them discuss price or anything. That's weird for an antique store, because you always haggle. It's expected, in most places."

"You didn't see him pay for it?"

Fisher shook his head. "I only saw him ask for the box. I recognized him and went into the first booth. I heard a bag rustle, and then I went to get JD. I never saw him pay, but I definitely didn't hear him haggle either." He wasn't sure if he was being helpful or not.

"But you didn't hear the register?" Detective Cloud asked.

"No, I didn't."

"I checked it as we left and heard another customer bring up an item," JD interjected. "The register drawer makes a ding when it opens. It wasn't quiet, and I think Fisher would have heard if it had been rung up. It's an old piece of equipment."

"What about the other day? At the same store."

"I was there with JD, and we saw this guy come in and ask for a vase. He said he'd called about it, just like Armand did. He was handed the vase from behind the counter, and then he left. I don't remember if he paid for it or not. I thought it really strange that someone would make such a big deal over a cheap knockoff that was probably made a few weeks ago in China."

"Is that what he bought?"

"Yeah. It was a cheap piece that anyone could buy anywhere. Why would anyone call to make sure it was saved for them? I can take you to the antique mall and show you half a dozen of them at least." Fisher turned to JD and then back to Red. "Is that all you wanted?"

"I'd like to know how you know Armand."

Fisher shook his head. "I won't answer any more questions," he said firmly. "I've helped you all I can, and now I want to go home." He was tired and still nervous as hell. That wasn't going to pass until he was out of the police station.

"Do you really think someone is using that store as a cover?" JD asked.

Fisher nodded. "Given what I saw and what I know about Armand, I'd say it's a good possibility. How you intend to prove it is another matter. I'm willing to bet they have plans in place if you walk in in uniform, and if someone they don't know starts using their code, they'll pack it up and move."

"We'd thought of that," Red said, standing. "We appreciate you coming in to tell us what you saw. It's a big help."

"Let's go," JD said.

Fisher followed him out to the car. JD drove them back to his house, where he let his mother inside, and then they rode to Fisher's apartment building. It was nearly dark by the time JD parked and they walked to the front door. He let himself in and cautiously climbed the stairs. He'd half expected his apartment to be boarded up, but he had a new door and hardware. Of course, his key no longer worked and he had to go to the first floor to the on-site manager to get it.

"I hope everything is okay," he said to himself and unlocked the door. Inside, everything seemed in one piece. He slowly stepped in as if the carpet had been mined or something. "It looks okay."

"I didn't see anything broken or moved. I think they were here for just a few minutes, and when you weren't, they set about waiting for you. It's good you left right away." JD hugged him as spasms of shaking went through Fisher.

"I hate that they were in here," he said softly. "They should leave me alone. I never did anything to hurt them. They're like the bullies on the playground. They never stop, and they seem to feel that whatever they want is theirs for the taking."

"Were you bullied a lot?" JD asked.

"All the time. I was gangly, awkward, and quiet. So I was an easy target. How about you?"

"No. I didn't have that problem. I was one of the popular kids. I had a few people decide to push me around, but I had friends, and we stood up for each other, so they backed off pretty fast. I figure that high school is a team sport. If you're going to survive unscathed, you have to have all the positions filled."

Fisher nodded. He didn't know anything about that. It had been just him against the world, or that was how it had felt at the time. "I want to see the bedroom."

He walked to the other room, opened the door, and breathed a sigh of relief. There was none of the mess he'd kept imagining, and his room smelled as fresh and clean as it always did. The bathroom was the same.

"Do you want to stay here tonight?" JD asked. "You're welcome to get some clothes and come home with me if you'd feel better."

Fisher wanted to take JD up on his offer, but he needed to be home and try to get over the sense that someone else had been here. Putting it off wouldn't help. "I need to stay here."

"Okay." JD leaned closer and kissed him lightly. "You have my number. Call if you need anything, and I'll hurry right over." JD squeezed his hand and then, after saying good-bye, he left the apartment.

Fisher closed and locked his new front door and then went from room to room, looking at everything. In the kitchen he opened and scrutinized all the drawers and cabinets. In the bedroom he examined his closet and checked out his dresser drawers. Then he was back in the kitchen, surveying the food in the refrigerator. In the end he decided it was fine. Then he thought about his car. So he opened the door, checked the hallway for strangers, and hurried to the back of the building and peered out the landing window. His car sat in the space where he'd left it and looked okay.

He went back inside, locked the door, and leaned against it. He didn't have to go to work until Tuesday, so he had some time to himself. After cleaning up and showering, he climbed into bed. He lay under his covers... listening. Sounds from the hall made him tense until they passed. A car outside rattled down the street. Fisher lay still, knowing he needed to sleep, but he stayed wide awake, jumping at any strange sound. And there were plenty. Four times before midnight he had his phone in his hand to call JD, but each time he stopped himself because he knew he was being stupid. He should feel safe in his own apartment. What scared him was that to really feel safe, he needed JD. He had to get over that.

At one thirty, after lying in bed for hours, he got up and pulled out the handled container of cleaning supplies. He started in the bathroom, cleaning all the fixtures and the tub. Moving on to the kitchen, he cleaned everything in there, including wiping out the cupboard under the sink. When he actually thought about running the vacuum at three in the morning, he knew he was going too far and put everything away and got out his broom, then swept all the floors. He thought about mopping, but decided to try going back to bed.

His apartment smelled of pine and it was clean. He'd managed to rid the place of any sign or scent that other people had been there. Then and only then was he able to close his eyes. Everything was quiet, and he finally fell into a light sleep, still ready to wake and run at the slightest sign of trouble.

CHAPTER
Seven

"WAS THAT woman who came in with you and Fisher really your mother?" Red asked the following day as JD came into the locker room at work.

"Yes. She and Fisher seemed to really get along. I saw them talking a lot, and my mother lost that pinched expression of disgust she always seems to direct my way."

"Is your mother staying long?" Red asked as he shrugged into his uniform shirt.

"She's already left for the airport. Her flight is in an hour." JD was of two minds about that. The feeling that he needed to constantly be on his guard was exhausting, but they had talked more in the last two days than they had in a long time. He didn't know if his mother's attitude was thawing permanently or not, but he was hopeful that time would eradicate some of the hurt and fear his parents had. And none of that would have happened without Fisher smoothing the way.

He changed into his uniform and checked the roster for his assignment. All it read was *Cloud*. "I guess I'm with Aaron today."

"We both are. He wants us to look into this antique store angle and see if there really is a connection to drug shipments and distribution." Red sat on the bench next to him. "Think about it. No one would think twice about traffic coming in and out, and there are large items to hide things inside. Besides, who thinks of an antique store as a nefarious place? Pawn shops, the secondhand places, some of the convenience stores that stay in

134

business, but we wonder how that's possible. Those we keep an eye on as closely as we can, but an antique mall?"

"Have we traced the owners?" JD asked.

"I don't know." Red stood, and JD finished dressing. They both checked in the mirror before leaving the locker area to find Detective Cloud.

"We're in here," he said as they approached one of the small conference rooms. "I thought we'd start with ideas.

"Do you really think there's something to this?" JD asked.

"I've had my suspicions about that place for a while. I don't see how a business filled with that much junk can survive. They basically try to sell the stuff everyone else would throw away."

"You aren't an antique person, then," JD commented.

"Doesn't matter. What your friend said last night made sense. And we have a known dealer at the location. That's enough for us to look into it."

"JD asked if we've traced ownership," Red said.

"I have Carter on that now. Let's see who's behind the business. Maybe that will tell us something."

"The real issue is how do we get proof?" JD said. "Do you have a plan?"

"That's the real shits. We can't go in there and start watching the place because then everyone will stay away."

"Do we know who the employees are?" JD asked. "Some of them have to be in on this. They can't be innocent bystanders. Fisher said that the first time, with the vase, his ex's new boyfriend was behind the counter. He wasn't there yesterday, so we know at least two people are involved."

"Get his name," Aaron said, writing down notes as they talked. JD did the same. "We might get someone to roll if we can corner them."

"Not if one of them is the main distributor. They're going to be scared as hell of him." JD continued taking notes.

"What we really need is someone on the inside."

"How are we going to do that? Have someone try to get a job there? That isn't going to work because they'll be suspicious of anyone new, and if the manager or owner is the kingpin, he'll only hire people he knows."

"Is there a camera system in the store?" Red asked, and JD wished he'd thought of that. "If there is, we may be able to tie into it somehow, especially if it's wireless. Intercepting the communications shouldn't be too hard."

"That might work. If they have one," Aaron said.

"I'll check on it," JD volunteered.

"Okay, what else?" Aaron prompted. "Would your friend be able to help us?"

"Fisher?" JD said. "He isn't a police officer, and I think he's done enough." He didn't want Fisher put in danger. If drugs were being distributed through the store, then the people who worked there were likely dangerous. JD had signed up for an element of risk when he became a police officer. Fisher hadn't.

Carter opened the conference room door and handed a page to Aaron. "Sit down." Aaron said to him, and Carter slid into the seat next to JD. "It seems that the owner of the store is Northside Antiques, Incorporated. That tells us nothing."

"No. It's a corporation, owned by another company, Antiques Unlimited, and they own another company, Antiques on the Pike, Inc. Sound familiar?" Carter asked.

"They own the place a few miles down the road as well," Red observed. "That means if both stores are involved, we'll need to get South Middleton involved."

"Yeah. I love these jurisdictional issues. For now we'll concentrate on the store in our jurisdiction and keep an eye on the other one. I'll call a friend in South Middleton PD and see if Antiques on the Pike is on their radar. They might be building a case from their end." Aaron made his own notes. "What else?"

"Do we want to spook them?" Carter asked.

"Not yet. We need to get to the bottom of this distribution network, and this is the first solid lead we have. I'd like to figure out how the communication works between them so we could use that to our advantage."

"Let JD and me work on that," Red said. "That might be something Fisher can help with."

"Then bring him in," Aaron said.

"If last night is any indication, he isn't going to talk to you. But he will to JD and me. Fisher isn't a suspect."

"I'd like to know how he knew Armand Dissant."

JD opened his mouth to say something, but Red beat him to it. "I don't know why you have a bee in your bonnet about Fisher, but you need to drop it or we aren't going to get the help we need."

"I know there's something going on between the two of you." Aaron looked right at JD. "You need to make sure you know the people you're allowing in your life. He has a record, and it's not pretty. Have you seen it?"

"You pulled his record?" JD asked, standing up as anger flowed through him.

"Of course I did. He was at the scene of a shooting, acting strangely. I needed some context and—"

"Was there anything recent?" JD challenged.

"No, but that doesn't mean anything," Aaron said.

"Other than he's trying to turn his life around," JD countered. "Leave him alone. He helped us both yesterday and at the shooting." Aaron couldn't argue with that. "You said yourself that he was helpful, so let it go." He got louder than he intended, and Aaron glared at him, but he didn't back down. Aaron had no right to try to dictate JD's personal life.

"Guys," Red said. "We need to check on those items we have and keep an eye out. What we need is more information. Maybe Carter could go with JD and see if they have a surveillance system and how open it is. I think I'm going to change clothes and pay the store a visit to see what I can see. Who knows? We may get lucky."

"Don't count on it, but it's a good idea," Aaron said. "Get the lay of the land, and I'll call my buddy and see what I can get from him."

JD left the room, with Carter following. "You know we can only get so close in a police car, and that's going to limit my ability to assess their system."

"I'll check out an unmarked car, change into civvies, and then we'll take us a ride," JD said, and a few minutes later they were driving through town. JD pulled into the parking lot of the small restaurant next door to the antique store and kept the engine running. "See what you can get."

"What are you going to do?" Carter asked, already typing at the computer resting on his lap.

"I was going to get a snack. That will give us an excuse to be here, and no one watching will pay us any mind." He got out and walked inside the small restaurant. He got some fries and sodas to go, then carried them back to the car. "Find anything?" JD asked as he put Carter's soda in the holder for him.

"They have a system, and it's not very secure. Anyone with a PC could hook into it. They have public Internet, and they're running it right through that, so it's basically open to the world. If you know where to look—and I do." Carter punched a few keys, and the inside of the store flashed on his screen. "I can only get what's happening at this moment. It would be nice to get what happened when Fisher was in the store, but there's nothing to stop us from watching."

"Why would they be so open?"

"It's a mistake lots of people make. They think 'out of sight, out of mind.' If they can't see it, then others can't either."

"What do we do? We can't sit here all the time and watch your screen. And won't the connection fade if we get too far away?"

"Yes. But at least we can have eyes inside the building should we need them. We should also ask for guidance as to whether we need a warrant for this. It is open to anyone passing by. Heck, it's close to them putting their security footage on the Internet. So it could be one of those gray areas."

JD groaned. He hated gray areas—it was where they usually got snagged. "I suppose as long as we didn't plan to use it as evidence, we might be able to watch. At least there's no sound, so we don't get into federal wiretapping issues." He ate his fries and watched the screen while Carter did the same. "I'm going to wander inside and see if anything is going on. It will also be a chance to find blind spots."

"All right."

JD got out and closed the door, casually walked across the parking lot, and went into the store. As they'd seen in the video, there were two people in the store other than him, one leaning on each side of the counter.

"I get off at six," the guy behind the counter said.

JD realized that he had to be Fisher's ex's boyfriend. He remembered him from before. JD waved and continued back into the store. The two men continued talking. JD was pleased that their voices carried in the quiet of the store.

"Good. I'll meet you at your place, and we can go out." That was the other man.

"Did I tell you your ex was in here the other day? He bought a cheap silver tea set." JD's hearing perked up. "What a dweeb. He looked as out of it as you always said he was."

"Fisher is crazy—even his own mother thinks so."

JD searched for a name and remembered *Gareth*. He hated the guy instantly and wanted to beat the crap out of him then and there.

"He was with another guy. A really hot one, if you ask me."

"Shit," JD mumbled under his breath. What if the guy remembered him? He hadn't gotten too close to the counter, and of course his clothes were different. Besides, he was just looking around and didn't plan to buy anything. Hell, but what if they reviewed the security feed and recognized him? This was a bad idea.

"Fisher has a new boyfriend?" Gareth sounded intrigued, and JD smiled. He should regret treating Fisher the way he did.

"Yeah. Think about it. He's the one who's going to have to deal with all those issues," the boyfriend said cattily.

"Yeah," Gareth said, his voice lowering, and JD had to strain to hear. "I was never so shocked in my life when you told me all those things he'd done. I had actually been thinking of asking him to take me back."

"Sweetheart, who is better for you than me?"

JD wanted to retch and nearly dropped what he was holding. That son of a bitch. Not that JD wanted Gareth in Fisher's life, but the little weasel had made sure Gareth stayed away from Fisher, and most likely when Fisher needed support the most. JD wanted to knock both their heads together.

The door jingled as another customer came in, the sound loud enough that it rang in JD's ears after he'd been straining. "I'll talk to you later."

"Okay. I have to go anyway," Gareth said, and the door jingled again a few seconds later as JD saw him leave. He picked up a few items, looking them over in case anyone saw him.

"Do you have an item for me?" The voice was deep and rough, like the man had smoked way too many cigarettes. JD kept hold of the items he had and decided to see if he could take a closer look. He walked past the front desk, where the scent of cigarettes hung in the air, and he nearly coughed at the choking smell. He kept his head turned away from the desk even as he concentrated on seeing both men in his peripheral vision.

"Can I help you with anything?"

"No. I'm just looking," JD said, doing his best to remove his accent and speaking in a slightly lower register. He didn't want to be memorable at all. He was starting to wonder just how much business was being done though this store. He'd been in here three times, and each time something had happened. Maybe it was a coincidence, but JD got the suspicion that a number of transactions had to be taking place each day.

"What is it I was supposed to have?" the man behind the counter asked.

"A vase of some type that my chick wanted," the man with the deep, throaty voice said.

It was getting more and more difficult for JD to pretend he was a customer and stick around to listen in. He should have gotten out, but now he needed to buy something without raising suspicion. Leaving would only make him memorable. He'd screwed up this time, for sure. Either way, he'd made it so he wouldn't be able to come in here again, at least not right away.

"What color was it?"

"Red or something. It was supposed to be behind the front desk. I don't remember the details. She's the one who pays attention to this stuff." He coughed, and JD started to wonder if this really was a customer. He made his way around and set the items he'd been carrying back where they'd been and found a small piece of jewelry. It was costume, but sort of interesting. Maybe his sister would get a kick out of it.

"I'm sorry. I don't have anything set aside." The weasel began looking. "Have her call me, and I'll see if I can help her."

"Okay, thanks."

The man left, and JD carried his purchase to the desk. He watched the guy behind the counter, wishing he had some sort of name tag. Anger coursed through him, and when he handed over the money, it took all his restraint to keep from throttling him. When the weasel rang up the purchase, JD paid attention to the sound the register made and then left the store. Thankfully he didn't seem to have been recognized. He hurried across the parking lot and got into the car.

"I thought we were going to witness a buy while you were in there," Carter said with a grin.

"Yeah, but it didn't turn out that way. I think he was just a customer. However, I want to get an ID on the guy behind the counter. He's the one who handled the first transaction Fisher witnessed. Also, let's try to ID the first guy who was in there with him. They were pretty chummy, and maybe he'll lead us to something."

"Like boyfriends chummy?"

"Like Fisher's ex-boyfriend and his new squeeze Weasel Boy. But that has nothing to do with this." JD clenched his fists.

"I'm sure it doesn't," Carter said. "You didn't hear a name?"

"No. But Weasel Boy is the guy Fisher saw that first time." JD took a deep breath and released it slowly. "We could be all wrong about this, but my instincts are telling me we're on the right track. That place is full of dusty, old junk. When I was trying to look like I was browsing, I saw tons of items that hadn't been touched in months, maybe years. There was dust everywhere."

"So...."

"So if a business is healthy, things don't sit, or they're at least cleaned and moved. Nothing has been. It's just sitting there." Maybe he wanted something to be wrong so badly that he was seeing what wasn't there.

"You bought something," Carter said.

"Yeah. It was a pin for a few dollars. I spent enough time in there that I didn't want to just leave. But I can't go back in there for a while, not when Weasel Boy is working. I overheard him telling Gareth that Fisher had a hot new boyfriend. He saw me before, and I don't want him tying me to Fisher or the previous visit."

"Calm down. You don't scream cop, and you know the guy is gay, so if he recognizes you, hit on him. He has a boyfriend, so he should tell you to back off, but he'll also think you're in there because you like him." Carter closed the lid on his computer. "I think we can go now. Weasel Boy is bored enough that he's actually watching porn on the computer. So let's go, and we can tell the detective what we found out." JD put the car in gear and backed up, then pulled out onto the main road.

"Are you going to tell Fisher what you heard?" Carter asked after a few minutes.

"No. He doesn't need to hear that kind of—" JD hit the brakes harder than he needed to. "Son of a bitch. I nearly missed it altogether. Weasel Boy told Gareth some things about Fisher when Gareth was considering taking him back."

"Okay?"

"How would Weasel Boy know any dirt to tell?" JD asked. "I mean, Fisher said he didn't know who he was when he saw him and Gareth together a while ago. But obviously Weasel Boy knew Fisher well enough to have bad things to say about him."

"Maybe he made it up?" Carter suggested.

"Do you think so?" JD asked. He hated being wrong, but maybe he was leaping to conclusions.

"No. Even if he lied, there has to be a ring of truth to it somewhere or it wouldn't be believed," Carter said as they turned into the station parking lot. "I take it Fisher has told you some of the things that Weasel Boy might have said."

"Yeah. It wasn't pretty, and if I'm honest, it scared the shit out of me. He knows things no one should ever have to know. But I believe he's worked hard to change his life, and I need to remember that when—"

"—his past casts a shadow on the present?" Carter finished, and JD nodded. "How bad can it be?"

"That's just it. I think he doesn't remember a lot of it, and what he does scares him. He said that he's had memory lapses and that some things are gone." JD pulled into a spot and turned off the engine. Then he shifted to face Carter. "The other day when he was at that shooting on the north side, he doesn't remember how he got there. All he can tell me was that he thought his ex was after him, and he kept going. I looked it up, and that happens sometimes with bipolar people. They sink into themselves and don't register what's going on around them." That was enough about Fisher. "But I can't tell any of this to Aaron, because Fisher's story is not mine to tell."

"I'll do some digging and see if I can't come up with an identity for Weasel Boy. Maybe that will give us another lead." Carter opened the car door, and JD did the same. They needed to tell the detective what they'd found and suspected. JD hoped like hell he hadn't sent all of them on some wild goose chase because of a hunch. Granted, police acted on hunches all the time, and sometimes they paid off and sometimes they didn't. But pursuing his hunch seemed to lead back to Fisher in one way or another. No matter what happened, that had the potential to be both good and bad. JD would do what he could to protect Fisher, but his past kept coming up, and there could be only so much JD could do.

HE SPENT the rest of his shift working with Carter to try to dig up identities on each of the players. "Justin C. Van Groot." Carter said with a smile. "That's Weasel Boy's real name."

"How did you find it?" JD asked as he moved to look at Carter's screen. The man in the picture was younger, but it was definitely him.

"I took a guess at his age and started looking at yearbooks, and there we go. He graduated from Cumberland Valley in 2008. He's aged pretty well. Now let's see what Mr. Van Groot has been up to." Carter typed away, and soon they saw what they expected. "His juvenile record has been sealed, but we can get that opened if we need to. But it seems he didn't stop as a juvie. An arrest for possession, which he weaseled out of." Carter chuckled. "You certainly gave him an appropriate nickname. It seems he's been arrested a number of times and has always managed to get off somehow. Most of the charges weren't too serious. The last one was assault a few years ago, and the charges were dropped."

"This guy sounds like a real prince. Send this over to Aaron. He's going to want to see it."

"He sent a car over to the area of the store and has them monitoring the feed from their cameras, since we can't monitor the other store.

Hopefully we'll see something that will give us the last piece of probable cause we'll need to get a warrant." Carter continued typing.

JD went to get lunch, since they'd definitely earned it, and afterward spent the time on edge, doing paperwork and hoping they'd get the go-ahead. By the time his shift ended, he was still in a holding pattern, so he changed and left the station, then drove right to Fisher's.

He rang the bell and was buzzed into the building. Fisher met him at the door with bags under his eyes. "What's wrong?"

"I didn't sleep well," Fisher said as JD looked around. Everything in the apartment sparkled, and he couldn't see a speck of dust anywhere. Even the sofa pillows had been furniture showroom fluffed and placed.

"Oh, honey," JD said as he eased them both inside. "You need to try to relax."

"I kept hearing sounds outside and then in the hall. Each time I wondered if it was people coming to get me." Fisher yawned and tried to turn away.

"Go get a blanket and a pillow and meet me on the sofa." JD kissed Fisher lightly and then waited for him to leave the room. JD removed the throw pillows and set them on the other chair. "Put the pillow down there and lie down." He sat at the end of the sofa, letting Fisher stretch his legs over his lap. He covered Fisher with the blanket and pulled off his socks before slowly rubbing his feet to keep them warm and to ease away the tension.

Fisher had soft skin, and JD was gentle. He didn't have lotion, so he kept the pressure light and soothing, watching as Fisher relaxed onto the pillow and made the same soft, satisfied moan as he did during certain amorous activities. "That feels so good."

"I know, honey. It's supposed to." JD continued rubbing, calming Fisher even as he was strung tight as a violin. This whole case and Fisher's involvement had him on edge.

"What's going on?" Fisher asked.

"I'm waiting for a call to raid the store," he answered as calmly as he could. "I want all of this over so you can feel safe again." And so Fisher's past could stay there, and if they decided to build a life together, they could do so in peace. He was jumping ahead impatiently, the way he always did. Even in his own mind there was little patience for anything that he wanted.

"What is it you want from me?" Fisher asked.

JD's tension ratcheted up a notch. This had always been the step when things fell apart. Before, it had been JD asking the question, but this time it was Fisher. He hoped like hell the result wasn't going to be the same. "I want to give things a chance," he answered and waited.

"Why?" Fisher whispered. "There are better people than me."

"Maybe you don't see your own worth," JD countered. "You have a lot of strength inside you. I know it's there. I've seen it peek out. It certainly did with my mother. You earned her respect, and I think she came to like you. That's a big deal with her, and weak, small people are what she eats for lunch."

"Please...."

"I attended one of her garden parties, and every one of those society ladies had claws and fangs that would make a tiger cringe in fear. They used words and gossip to hurt, and Mom learned to be strong, to stand on her own, and then reign as queen bee. I may have taken that away from her, but not for long. So don't underestimate the impact you had on her."

"But my past.... And people are going to say that I'm with you for your money, especially when it gets around about what you inherited," Fisher said.

"One thing I learned from 'my disgrace,'" JD began as he made air quotes and then returned his fingers to Fisher's feet, "is that people will think what they want, and often the worst, but what counts is what you believe. The rest is pretty much crap."

Fisher chuckled softly, and JD rubbed the bottom of his feet a little harder, earning a soft, contented moan. "Is that what you believe?"

"Why is it so hard for you?" JD countered.

Fisher's eyes had drifted closed, but he opened them and sat up, pulling his feet away. "Because the people who were supposed to like me and care for me first and foremost pushed me away when things got hard. Yes, I was doing things that weren't good, I see that now, but instead of helping, all they wanted was to shove me aside because I was too much bother." Fisher looked pained. "How am I supposed to believe that anyone will like me or care for me, when they didn't?"

"You just have to believe that they were wrong," JD told him. It was the only answer he had, though he wished like hell he had a better one. "Self-worth has to come from inside. It can't come from anybody else."

"That's easy for you to say." Fisher pinned JD with his gaze. "Look at you. You're sex on a stick, and I'm a washed-up—"

JD leaned into Fisher's gaze, meeting it measure for measure. "You're full of shit. You're anything you allow yourself to be. All this 'poor me' stuff is crap, or it can be if you let it go. You are who you are, the same as the rest of us, and yes, you have more challenges than most, but so what? That doesn't make you less than anyone else, and it doesn't mean you can't be loved if you're willing to open your heart to it."

"How can you say that? Look what your parents did to you."

"And I left and moved on. So did you." JD wasn't going to cut Fisher any slack, not about this. He knew he was right. Fisher needed to give himself more credit, and it pissed JD off that he didn't. "You built a new life. Don't underestimate that. It takes a lot of courage do what you did, and I've seen plenty of people who couldn't. Now lie back down and relax." He waited, and when Fisher rested back on the pillow, JD started on his feet and legs again. "You can answer my first question if you want."

"You're like a dog with a bone," Fisher said, and JD tilted his head slightly. "Yes. I want to see what happens between us. But I'm scared of getting hurt."

"Because of Gareth the Wanker?" He loved that he could use the Britishism. "He was an idiot. Look who he's dating now and think about what's going to happen to him. You are so much better off, because no matter what he says, if he's mixed up in what's going on at the store, he's going down in a big way." JD rubbed a little harder, and Fisher finally began to relax again. "The man doesn't have the world's best decision-making skills."

"I'll give you that," Fisher agreed and closed his eyes once again. JD stopped talking and let the room grow quiet. Soon Fisher's breathing evened out, and JD slowed and then stopped his foot massage, letting

Fisher sleep. They both needed it, and JD rested his head back on the cushions and nodded off for a few minutes.

JD woke when Fisher stirred. He lifted Fisher's legs and gently placed them back on the sofa after he got up. Working out the crick in his neck as he walked, JD pushed aside the curtains and peered out at the street below.

"What are you doing?" Fisher asked. "The street out there isn't that interesting. I've stared at it plenty of times."

"I thought you were asleep. I didn't want to wake you." JD let the curtains fall back into place and joined Fisher back on the sofa. This time he sat near his chest, and Fisher pulled him downward.

Languid kisses lasted and soon grew more heated and energetic. JD's wondering if Fisher wanted more was answered when Fisher slid out from under him and extended his hand. JD stood, and Fisher took it, leading him to the bedroom.

There were times for frantic, wild, athletic sex. This wasn't one of them as far as JD was concerned. Oh, the room filled with Fisher's moans as JD filled his mouth with his lover's length. He tasted and teased until Fisher shook and groaned at the top of his lungs. He'd give anything to hear those sounds each and every day.

"You make me want things I never dreamed," JD whispered as he claimed Fisher's lips once again.

"Me?"

"Yes," JD answered with another kiss. "You." He pulled back, raking his gaze over Fisher, trying to make him understand how beautiful he was. Long and lean, smooth, a body of a real man without being primped, pumped, or landscaped. Fisher was as he came, as God made him, and that was incredibly beautiful. It wasn't likely that anyone was going to be using Fisher as the model for a statue, but he'd be perfect. If they did, JD would be jealous because he wanted to be the only one to look at Fisher.

"What about the guy back in Charleston?"

"Bobby? He and I were.... I loved him, but it's not the same with you."

"Did you love him more?" Fisher asked.

"No. Just different. Bobby was.... It's hard to explain. He was the heady kind of love, where with you, it's different and feels deeper." JD swiped his thumb over Fisher's lips. "Don't say anything. I know what I just told you, and you don't need to say anything back. When you're ready you can say anything you like, but for now just be happy."

Fisher smiled and inhaled raggedly. JD kissed him again, afraid Fisher was going to cry, and he didn't want tears at a time like this. He didn't want Fisher to remember crying, so he concentrated on driving Fisher crazy, filling the room with his moans again. When he entered Fisher a little while later, to a long, drawn-out groan, Fisher rolled his head back and forth on the pillow and arched his back. "Jay... Dee...." Nothing said sex as much as the way he drew out his name.

JD held Fisher close to him, rocking slowly, moving together as he sank into Fisher's deep blue eyes while Fisher's body gripped around him. "I want you to come around me."

"JD, I...," Fisher said breathlessly as JD straightened up and took Fisher's cock, stroking it slowly and firmly while he continued the slow rolls of his hips. Damn, he was trying to make sure Fisher climaxed. But it was hard to concentrate on anything but the look of him as he lay beneath him, Fisher breathless, a slight sheen of sweat, and damn if his eyes didn't shine with an inner light that JD knew had been doused for a while. That alone was exciting, but add to it the way Fisher responded to him, and JD's head spun. He stroked faster, harder, making Fisher writhe, sending sensation after sensation through him. JD's own body betrayed him, and he could no longer contain his excitement. He came hard, filling the condom, and seconds later Fisher followed.

The flush of Fisher's cheeks and the slight curl of his lips said a lot. JD slowly stroked Fisher's cheek, holding the rest of his body still, so they'd remain connected as long as possible. When he backed away, he did so reluctantly and then quietly left the room, took care of cleanup, and returned to help Fisher before rejoining him in bed.

Fisher finally slept next to him, relaxed and calm. JD held him and listened as Fisher snored softly in his ear, sharing the warmth as the wind picked up, whistling outside the window. Eventually, JD carefully extricated himself to get a drink. He pulled on his underwear and wandered into the living room. As he finished and put his glass in the sink, his phone rang. JD hurried back to the bedroom and pulled it out of his pants pocket.

"Red," he said as he answered.

"Get to the station as fast as possible if you want to be part of this."

"Okay," he said and ended the call. He pulled on his pants and shirt and sat on the edge of the bed to put on his socks and shoes. The bed vibrated and then JD was held in Fisher's bare arms, the warmth seeping through his clothes. "I have to go in. The raid is going down." JD felt Fisher nod, but he didn't say anything. "I'll be okay."

"You can't promise that," Fisher said and tightened his hold. "I know you have to go, but I don't want you to."

JD stopped and turned around. "I know what I'm doing, and I'll take every step to be safe. The guys will also be there, and we'll watch each other's backs." JD leaned in, kissed Fisher as hard and deep as he could, then leaned back. "I have to go right away." The worry in Fisher's eyes nearly stopped him but he didn't want to be late. That wasn't him, and JD pulled on his last sock and got into his shoes. "I'll call you as soon as I can." He took a final glance at Fisher, hating the fact that he had to leave him and how vulnerable Fisher looked crouched on the bed, naked. He wanted to reassure him, but instead he left the room and grabbed his coat. "I promise I'll call." JD pulled open the apartment door and closed it after himself. He didn't wait to see if Fisher locked the door; he didn't have time.

When he reached the top of the stairs, his coat was on and he was ready. JD turned and saw Fisher in the doorway of his apartment, a robe wrapped tightly around him. He wanted to rush back and hold him, to tell Fisher that everything would be all right. But he didn't have any more moments to spare, so he turned and raced down the stairs.

CHAPTER *Eight*

FISHER CURLED up on the sofa after picking up his phone. He shivered under the blanket and pulled it up to his neck. The door was closed and locked, and he was safe in his own apartment, he hoped. He placed his phone on the small table next to him and made sure it wasn't on silent. Then he turned on the television and put on one of the local channels, hoping if there was some real news they would cover it. He kept the volume low and watched mostly because he needed something to do.

His nerves were out of control. Fisher shook as he tried not to think about what could be happening to JD. If Red, Carter, and Kip were there, then he knew their partners would be just as worried as he was. Maybe they got used to it over time. But somehow he doubted it, because Fisher doubted he ever could do that. Waiting like this was something he would never be good at.

A sharp sound outside made him jump. It was a car, not a shot, but it ramped up his tension further. He wished he could call one of the other guys, but he didn't have their numbers, so he watched the television and tried with all his might not to imagine what could be happening to JD at that moment. He had no way of knowing, and at one point he considered getting dressed and driving to that side of town just so he could see what was going on. Of course he realized that was totally stupid and stayed where he was. He thought about getting something to eat, but the thought of food had his stomach roiling, so he gave up on that idea.

After an hour, Fisher did get dressed. What if something happened and he had to help JD? He couldn't leave the apartment in his robe, so he cleaned up, dressed, and then sat once again on the sofa, watching the television. Finally the evening programming was interrupted.

"Carlisle police have raided a business suspected of distributing illicit narcotics," the anchor, a young man with perfectly combed hair and blinding white teeth, said seriously. "We'll have more details as they become available." The station went back to their regular programming, and Fisher swore at the screen before returning to his vigil. He tried looking online, but could find no additional information.

Another hour passed, and he was becoming frantic.

"More on that shootout with police in Carlisle, right after these messages," the television announcer said, and Fisher sat on the edge of his seat as commercial after commercial played on. Finally they returned to the news program and the studio announcer cut to another reporter on the scene.

"This is Terry Digger. I'm on the north side of Carlisle on the Harrisburg Pike, where a shootout at an antique store has left one officer injured, and two shooters from inside the store are in custody. Police aren't saying at this time why the Northside Antique Mall was raided by police or why the men inside had so much weaponry, but neighbors are saying that they have suspected the business was a front for drugs for some time."

"Then why in the hell didn't they say something?" Fisher yelled at the screen. "Dumbasses."

"We're here with the detective in charge. Detective Cloud, can you tell us what happened?" The reporter tilted the microphone to the detective, who gave a very factual and vague account of what had happened and why they were there. He didn't give many details. He confirmed the injury of one officer but didn't give a name. Fisher was going crazy, and then his phone rang. It was a strange number, but Fisher snatched it up.

"Fisher, it's JD. I'm fine. My phone got damaged, and I couldn't call earlier, but I'm okay. Red was hurt, and they're taking him to the hospital to be patched up."

"Was he shot?" Fisher asked as relief washed over him.

"Yes. But his vest took the brunt of it. The force sent him to the ground, and he hit his head. So they're taking him in. It doesn't seem to be severe, but we're going to make sure. I have some wrap-up to do here and reports to write, and then I'll be back."

"Did you eat?"

"I'll grab something at the station," JD told him. "But you need to eat and relax a little. I have to go, but I'll be home as soon as I can." JD hung up, and Fisher set his phone by the sofa, breathing a sigh of relief. JD was fine and he'd be back soon. At least Fisher hoped so. He turned off the television and went to the kitchen to make a little dinner.

JD arrived at his door hours later, tired and dragging. Fisher helped him in and gave him something to drink before leading him right to the bathroom, where he got JD in the shower and his dirty clothes in his bag. Once JD came out with only a towel around his waist, Fisher pushed aside his instantly strident libido and settled him into bed, sans the towel. JD was asleep within minutes, and Fisher lay down into bed next to him, cuddled up against him, and closed his eyes. It was time to rest; there would be plenty of time to deal with his fears.

"JD, DON'T you have to go to work?" Fisher asked the following morning when he woke and saw that it was nearly nine o'clock and JD was still curled next to him in bed.

"Nope. Got the day off. Worked too many hours," JD answered groggily and tugged him back down under the covers. "Sleepy. Need rest."

"Okay," Fisher said happily and settled back to rest against him. He wasn't tired, but if JD wanted to cuddle awhile, who was he to deny alone time in bed with his hunky cop boyfriend? That thought put a smile on his face that lingered even after the memories of the night before returned to him. "I should make breakfast," he said a few minutes later when JD's belly made its presence known with a rumble.

"I guess I didn't have much dinner," JD mumbled as he rolled over, unburying his head from the covers.

"Then I'm going to cook, and you can come out in a while." Fisher hopped out of bed, smiling as JD reached for him. He pulled on his robe and slippers, then went out to the kitchen to see what he had. "I hope bagels are okay."

He didn't get an answer, and when he peered into the bedroom, JD was fast asleep again, his head on Fisher's pillow, body and arms sprawled out over the entire bed. He decided to let him sleep and popped some bagels in the toaster, poured glasses of juice, and got out a package of cream cheese. Fisher set everything on the table and returned to the bedroom. JD hadn't moved.

"I got some food ready."

Slowly JD rolled over and got out of bed, shivering at the chill in the air. Fisher pressed to his perfect backside and wound his arms around JD's belly. "Warmer?"

"Much." JD pressed Fisher's hands lower—part of him was definitely wide awake.

"I cooked, sort of, and if you want to eat, we need to now. There will be plenty of time to take care of Mr. Happy." Fisher got his summer robe from the closet and handed it to JD. It wasn't as warm as the one he was wearing now, but it would be better than JD freezing off important parts.

JD joined him at the table.

"What happened last night?" Fisher asked, trying not to shake as he spread cream cheese on his cinnamon raisin bagel.

"You were right. The place was being used to distribute drugs, but it was so much bigger than that. The basement walls were lined with shelves of every kind of illicit drug, I swear. The damn place was a drug warehouse. There were pills of all kinds, powders, crystal, more of some than others. When we got the dogs near the place, they went nuts. We captured both men inside, including Weasel Boy. Gareth's current boyfriend. We think he was in charge, and he was armed to the teeth. He's the one who fired on Red, but one of the other officers put a gun to his head, and he came to his senses."

"Was Gareth there?" Fisher breathed.

"No. We have officers out looking for him. Not that Weasel Boy turned on him, but he's been in the store, and we are going to want to talk to him."

Fisher got the idea that there was going to be much more than talking when they found Gareth. "He wasn't a bad guy when I knew him."

"How can you say that after what he did?" JD asked angrily, putting down his bagel.

"What happened to me wasn't pretty, and yeah, maybe things wouldn't have gotten so bad if one by one everyone hadn't turned away. But maybe I needed to hit rock bottom so I'd realize what was happening and try to change my life. I don't know. But the Fisher you know isn't the same one he knew. I'm different now. I don't like him, and I'm definitely not going to be friends with him, but I didn't want this for him either."

"Whatever happens, remember that he brought it on himself. You aren't to blame for the decisions Gareth made in his life."

"I know," Fisher said, basking a little in JD's concern. "I was angry with him for so long, focusing on him as a source of rage and hurt. But none of that matters now, and what happens, happens. I don't want to be involved in that. I haven't for a while. The life I had was dark, but now I see light and brightness even on a day like today."

Fisher turned toward the windows, where gray light filtered in and flakes of snow fell on the other side. He returned to eating and finished his breakfast, very content for the moment to watch JD and the way the robe Fisher had given him didn't quite seem to fit.

"So what happens with all the stuff you found?" Fisher asked to keep his mind on something other than the way JD's chest kept peeking out more and more from between the folds of the light blue robe.

"It will be seized and put under extreme lock and key as evidence. We're going to try to get as much information as we can about the organization and who was behind it." JD grinned. "We found plenty of records and names in the store. They were hidden among the store records and in the store computer. I suspect that Weasel Boy is going to want to make a deal because he isn't going to last very long otherwise."

"Why?"

"He may not have talked, but the information he left to be found, which should have been destroyed, will do the talking for him. How he got into this business is a bit puzzling. He did dumb things and thought he'd never be caught."

"How long do you think this had been going on?"

"Quite a while, from the looks of things. Maybe two to three years, could be longer, since he probably started small and worked his way up. You did see a couple drug pickups, but not the payoffs. Other people brought in merchandise for sale, and Weasel Boy bought it and paid them wads of cash. There were codes and amounts, depending on the kind of item asked for. We could have bugged the phones and apparently everything would have sounded like normal antique store business." JD ate the last of his breakfast and sat back. "It seems that was what he was afraid of, having his phone bugged."

"Was he using?"

"I don't know. When he set this up, probably not, but he could have been over time. He had everything, and what's to say he didn't pop a few pills to feel better or keep going. They'll figure it out soon enough." JD stood and cleared the table. "I'm going to call Terry to see how Red is doing."

"I'll finish here and then go in to get dressed." It was over. Hopefully there wouldn't be people trying to break into his apartment any longer. It was likely they would be lying low and waiting out this latest burst of attention. The best part of all of this was that he got JD. Fisher did the dishes with a smile. He'd done some good. He'd been able to help JD in his job. As he worked, he heard JD's voice while he talked on the phone. When he heard laughter, he knew Red was going to be okay, and another point of worry evaporated.

Fisher was happy; he felt it bubble up from inside him. As he thought about it, he realized that he had almost everything he could want. Yes, there were things in his life that were disappointing, but he'd learned to live without them, and he'd continue forward. The difference now was that he didn't have to do it alone. JD had told him that he loved him, even made love to him, and he was going to believe in that and hold on to it.

Fisher finished up what he was doing and then joined JD in the bedroom. He found him sitting on the side of the bed. JD said good-bye and ended his call.

"Red's going to be fine, and apparently Aaron called this morning to find out how he was doing and told him that they're rounding up dealers and suppliers all over town. Carter decoded information on the computers, and raids have been happening at a number of locations. It's a real housecleaning." JD reached out and snatched Fisher, pulling him between his legs. "That's a good thing, but I have something much nicer that I'd like to talk about."

Fisher quivered as JD ran his hands up his legs and under the robe to cup and massage his ass. "This is a much better subject," JD said as he drew his hands away and opened the knot in the front of Fisher's robe. Then he slid his hands up along the seam of the robe, gently tugging it off Fisher's shoulders until it slipped off his arms and fell to the floor.

Fisher flushed, instantly hotter than he should be, as JD shucked his own robe, sitting in front of him naked, cock pointing up in his direction. Fisher pressed JD back on the bed, intent on looking at him for a few minutes, but JD had other ideas, tugging him down into a deep kiss.

JD stroked down his back and over his ass, cupping his cheeks and then teasing his opening with the tip of his finger until Fisher broke the kiss to groan loudly, pressing back into the sensation. "Let's you and I talk about something amazing and sexy for a few hours."

"Uh-huh," Fisher agreed, unable to think clearly.

"Then we can figure some other things out between us if you want."

Fisher nodded vigorously, losing himself in the sensation. Talking wasn't what he needed right now. Action was called for, and he figured JD was more than up for it. He crawled up on the bed and tugged JD on top of him. "Just so you know, I'm going to hold you to that 'few hours' you were talking about."

JD leered at him. "That's fine, sweetheart. Now roll over onto your stomach so I can show you just how much you mean to me. Put those hands up against the headboard and hang on. You're going to heaven." Fisher did what JD told him to, nerves kicking up ever so slightly until JD trailed his fingers up his legs. Then JD parted his cheeks and used that tongue of his to drive Fisher so high, he was looking at heaven in the rearview mirror.

"I THINK we're going to go out tonight," JD said the following Sunday, after they'd had another of their afternoon naps. "You've cooked and taken care of me this entire weekend. So I thought we'd walk on down to the pub for dinner. It being Sunday, that's about all that's open, but it will be nice and we can eat our fill." JD patted his very flat belly, and Fisher reached over, stroking the muscled ridges.

"Okay. We worked up an appetite. I'm going to get cleaned up and dressed." He started toward the bathroom. "What are you going to do?"

JD jumped off the bed, tugging Fisher close. "Join you." JD lightly pinched Fisher's butt, and he squealed and raced for the bathroom door with JD right behind him.

"You be good."

"Oh, I intend to be," JD rasped in his bedroom voice, which sent a ripple of desire down Fisher's back that pooled in his already hardening cock. Somehow they managed to make it into the bathroom and shower without falling or groping each other to death. And by the time the water had washed away the last of their passion, they were ready to dress and get something to eat. "Let's go build up our strength," JD added with a grin.

THE SNOW from the previous day had stopped and left the roads slushy. The sidewalks were clear and the air crisp and dry as Fisher burrowed under his coat, hat, and gloves while he and JD walked through town toward the English-style pub.

"We should have driven," JD said. "It's too cold."

"If this is going to be your home, then you'll need to get used to it." Fisher walked closer, taking JD's arm. "Besides, I'll warm you up later." He leaned on JD as they stopped at the light on the square, waiting to cross the street. The light changed and they crossed, continuing on toward the restaurant.

"You did this to me!" someone shouted from behind them. Fisher tensed and turned, wondering who was yelling. "This is all your fault." A man hurried toward them, pointing. "I know you did this, Fisher."

"JD, what's happening?" he asked as JD whirled around.

Gareth lumbered up to them.

"Gareth, go home."

"No home to go to," he retorted. "You ruined my life. You—somehow you took everything." Gareth came closer.

JD pressed Fisher back behind him. "Sir, you need to calm down. This isn't going to help." He was so calm it made Fisher feel better. JD was going to handle this, and he wasn't alone. "Just relax and go on back home. It's too cold to be out here."

"No home. The police took it. And it's all his fault." Gareth pointed at him again, and Fisher got a good look at his eyes, wild and huge. He knew that look; he'd seen it in the mirror more than once.

"Gareth, you aren't thinking clearly. You need to go home and take care of yourself," Fisher said gently, mimicking JD's tone as best he could. "That's what you need to do. Get some rest and take care of yourself."

"No. I need to make you pay. He said he saw you in the store. He said you were there and you know these things. You were a user. You were good for nothing, washed up, and then you were there, so you must have done this. He's in jail and you put him there," Gareth ranted on.

JD reached into his pocket at the same time Fisher did.

"No!"

"We're only getting you some help," JD said, fumbling for his phone.

"No!" Gareth yelled and reached into his coat pocket, then pulled out a gun. "I said no. You're going to pay." He pointed the gun at Fisher, who stood still, hoping like hell that JD knew what to do.

"There's no need for that. Fisher had nothing to do with whatever's bothering you. Now put the gun down before you do something you'll regret."

Cars drove by, and Gareth was far enough out of it that he didn't seem to realize they were in full view of anyone passing. Fisher realized that all they needed to do was try to keep Gareth calm and help would arrive… he hoped.

"No. He has to pay." Gareth began waving the gun, alternating between pointing it at JD and then him.

"He's high," Fisher whispered under his breath, hoping JD could hear him. He certainly didn't want Gareth to. "I never did anything to you," he said more loudly. "After I was injured, you left me. You said you wanted someone else, so you left. I've only seen you a few times since then. How could I do anything to you?" Fisher got more and more concerned about Gareth's behavior. He was teetering back and forth like an unstable building in a gale.

"You were there. Justin saw you. He said so. Pathetic Fisher was in the antique store, and now Justin's in jail. I know you had something to do with this. I left, and you had to get even, so you did all this, and now I'm going...." Gareth stopped and seemed to lose focus. Before Fisher could say anything, JD lunged, knocking Gareth to the ground.

"Get away," JD said as he fought a thrashing Gareth. Fisher backed away like JD said and pulled out his phone, calling 911 to say that there was a scuffle in progress on North Hanover, and that an off-duty police officer was involved. "He needs help. *Now.*" A shot reverberated off the building, just one. Fisher saw the gun skitter along the sidewalk and he hurried up, kicking it farther away. Then he looked at JD and felt the blood drain from his face as JD's coat darkened.

Fisher didn't know what happened next. The seconds blurred together, and soon he was being pulled away from Gareth, his aching hands held still. "Fisher, it's Carter. Are you okay?"

"He shot JD," Fisher said, trying to get back to Gareth.

"We got that. You were yelling it at the top of your lungs. Go see to JD while we take care of this guy."

Fisher calmed and nodded. Carter let him go, and he hurried to JD, who sat on the concrete holding his arm. "Son of a bitch shot me in the shoulder," JD said. "I'm going to be all right. There's an ambulance on the way."

"Okay." Fisher gulped for air and tried his best to calm himself. "I hear more sirens." Red and white lights confirmed that an ambulance was indeed approaching. As soon as they stopped, two men jumped out and began working on JD.

"What about him?" one of the EMTs asked, looking at Gareth. "He looks beaten pretty good."

"He'll be fine until you're done with him," Carter said, keeping Gareth on the ground. "Did you touch the gun?" Carter asked Fisher, who shook his head.

"Just kicked it out of the way. I don't know if JD touched it. He was struggling with Gareth, and then he shot him. He looked high to me. His speech was rambling, and he was wavering as he stood." He wasn't letting Gareth get away with anything.

"Did he get injured in the scuffle?" the EMT asked as he put a pressure bandage on JD's arm in preparation for transportation to the hospital.

"Maybe some." JD grinned. "Fisher went all protective on his ass. He sat on him, wouldn't let him up, and might have seen a little red. I'm not really sure." JD winked, and the other officers nodded in agreement.

"He's high enough he isn't going to feel anything for a little while longer."

Apparently a second ambulance was called, and they loaded Gareth into it, with police officers riding along. They loaded JD into the first ambulance, and Fisher climbed in as well, sitting in the only available space. "I'm not leaving him."

"Okay," Carter agreed. "But we will have to talk to you."

"We'll answer your questions later," JD said as they closed the ambulance doors. "You were something else," he said to Fisher. "You didn't panic, and you got rid of the gun and held Gareth down so he couldn't hurt me any longer."

"I went a little nuts," Fisher said.

"The thing is, you didn't shy away or panic. You did exactly what you had to do to protect me." JD reached for him with his good hand. "You had my back, and that was great."

"All I could think of was that I'd lost you." The ambulance started moving, and Fisher steadied himself. The siren wailed, and trying to speak over it wasn't very easy. He held JD's hand and brought it to his lips once. "I love you," Fisher said, and that JD heard. Fisher knew from the smile and the fact that JD mouthed, "I love you too" and then brought Fisher's hand to his own lips. "You're a tiger."

"I was terrified."

"So was I," JD said.

"Just lie back and try not to move," the EMT told JD. "We'll be at the hospital in a few minutes. They're expecting us and already have an area set up to receive you."

"Being scared isn't the issue. It's not letting the fear paralyze you so you can do the right things, and you did."

"Why did you jump at him?"

"I saw an opening, but he reacted faster than I thought he would. I had the gun away from him, but he lunged for it and the damn thing went off. I got it away from him in the end and then you took over."

"You saved me," Fisher said.

"And then you did the same. Never forget that. You were as brave and strong as anyone I've ever seen. And there was no panic or nervousness. You acted quickly to protect me." JD continued holding Fisher's hand as he closed his eyes, and they made the last of the journey to the emergency room.

After that things happened pretty fast. JD was taken out and inside. Fisher was escorted back once they got JD settled, and he sat in the chair next to where JD rested in a bed.

Nurses came in and set up IVs, attached monitors, and then after a few minutes, all of it was wheeled out so they could take JD for initial tests and X-rays. Fisher sat, his leg shaking, while he waited for them to return. JD returned ten minutes later, and a doctor followed him in. "Mr. Burnside, we're going to prep you for surgery so we can remove the bullet and repair any damage to your shoulder. The surgeon is on his way, and we're not going to wait."

JD nodded and said, "Okay. And please keep Fisher informed about how things are going."

The next hour was a whirl of activity. Fisher was shown to a surgical waiting room. Once JD was in surgery, Fisher wandered through the hospital to the cafeteria and got some coffee and food out of the machines, then returned to the waiting room. JD had given him his phone, but it was locked and he didn't have the code, so the numbers inside were lost to him. He managed to get a signal and took a chance, trying to look up the number of JD's parents online using his own phone. There were too many Burnsides, and he didn't know JD's father's name, so that was a dead end as well.

When JD's phone vibrated on the table in front of him, Fisher snatched it up. "Hello."

"Jefferson Davis?" a female voice asked.

"I'm sorry, this is his friend Fisher. Who is this?"

"His sister," she answered.

"Rachel? Thank God. JD was injured. He was shot in the shoulder, and he's in surgery right now. I tried to call Mary Lynn, but his phone is locked tight and I don't have the number." At least word would get back to JD's family.

"You know who I am?"

"Yeah. JD told me the story about taking you hunting." Fisher smiled briefly, but it faded as the worry returned.

"He would," she said, her accent light but lyrical. "Is JD going to be okay?"

"Yes. His life isn't in danger, but they need to remove the bullet and repair the damage. If you give me your number and your mother's, I'll call both of you when he's out of surgery."

She rattled off numbers at a frantic pace. Fisher punched them into his phone and read them back.

"What happened? Was it a robbery or something?" she asked.

"No. An ex-boyfriend of mine attacked us on the street, and JD protected me." Once again, he'd been the cause of pain for someone in his life. "I'm so sorry."

"What for? You didn't shoot him, did you?" Rachel countered. "If it was an ex doing things like that, it sounds like you made a good decision dumping the loser." Dang, Fisher was starting to like her already. "I'm sure Jefferson Davis would never blame you."

"No, he wouldn't."

"So are you my brother's new boyfriend?"

"He said I was," Fisher said.

"So you're the famous Fisher. My mother hasn't stopped talking about you since she got home. Apparently you made quite an impression, complete with telling her off. There are people in Charleston who would have bought tickets to see that, let me tell you." Good God, Fisher was starting to wonder how he could switch her off. She talked a mile a minute. "I can't wait for JD to bring you for a visit."

"Okay." Fisher wasn't sure what else to say.

"He'll have to come down to settle Aunt Lillibeth's estate, so I hope he brings you." She barely paused for breath. "You call me when he's out of surgery, and tell him I'm going to hound him something fierce until he calls me back."

"I will." Fisher was beginning to wonder if answering the phone had been a good thing or not. "Hopefully it should only be another hour or so. I'll pass on the messages." He ended the call and then dialed Mary Lynn's number. When it went straight to voice mail, he figured she was probably already on the phone with Rachel, but he didn't want to not call. He left a message and asked her to call him back on JD's phone.

"Rachel just told me," Mary Lynn said when she called him a few minutes later. "Is he all right?"

"He will be. Like I told Rachel, they had to remove the bullet and repair the damage to his shoulder. He'll have to heal and probably have therapy and things, but he should be fine. I'll call you and Rachel once he's out of surgery." This time he got off easy. Mary Lynn was pleased and kept the conversation short, but kind.

Once the phone calls were done, he sat back to wait. There was nothing more he could do except worry. He wondered where JD's friends were and figured they must still be cleaning up the shooting mess.

"Mr. Moreland," a woman said as she approached. "Mr. Burnside is out of surgery, and he's going to be fine. They removed the bullet and did some repair work on the bone and muscle. The surgeon said that given time Mr. Burnside should have full use of his shoulder."

"Thank you. Can I see him?"

"He's in Recovery. I'll take you back now. They're getting him settled, and later we'll find him a room. Mostly he's going to need rest and sleep."

"Thank you." Fisher followed her out of the waiting area and into a dimly lit room where JD lay on a bed, his shoulder heavily bandaged and his eyes closed. Fisher sat in the chair next to his bed. "I'm here," he said gently, lightly touching JD's fingers.

"Fisher," JD rasped.

"I'll bring him some ice chips," one of the Recovery nurses said and hurried away. When she returned she placed a cup on the tray and leaned over the bed, asking questions about JD's pain levels. Fisher stayed out of the way, and once they'd given JD something for pain, Fisher carefully fed him an ice chip.

"Just relax. I'm here. I talked to your mother and sister, and I'll call them soon and let them know how you are."

"You were wonderful," JD said.

"I think you have me mixed up. You're the one who took on the armed gunman to save me."

"Did they get him?"

"Yeah." Fisher wondered just how much Gareth was mixed up in this whole drug distribution organization. He had hoped Gareth had been an innocent bystander, but that was much less likely now. "He's at the hospital being checked out, as far as I know, and then I'm sure they'll haul him to jail. Your coworkers weren't about to cut him any slack." Fisher helped JD with another ice chip and then grew quiet. JD needed to rest, and they would have plenty of time to talk and figure things out.

They stayed in Recovery until JD was ready to be moved to his room. At that point he had a number of friends who popped in to check up on him. JD slept through all of it, but Fisher accepted their flowers, plants, and cards for him as well as called JD's mother and sister. Then, when he wasn't able to stay awake any longer, he said good-bye to JD and caught a ride with Red and Terry, who offered to drive him home. He hated to leave, but they were still working out the kinks at the new location, so he knew he'd be busy the next day at the warehouse.

"HOW ARE you feeling?" Fisher asked when he arrived in JD's room late the following afternoon, after another long day of straightening out system glitches and messes with the new facility. JD opened his eyes, and then Fisher saw it—a smile, warm and caring, the one JD always seemed to reserve especially for him. "I brought you your phone."

"I was wondering where it was."

"You have a bunch of messages, and your mother said that she was willing to come look after you. I told her it wasn't necessary. I can take perfectly good care of you."

"What did she say to that?"

"Believe it or not, she invited us for Christmas. *Us*," Fisher said. "She even said that she meant that you and I were specifically invited. I guess your mom's coming around. She said it was going to be a simple holiday this year. Whatever that means."

"Doesn't matter," JD said. "We can do whatever you like."

"I have vacation time saved up, and the actual holidays are slow for us. We usually gear up again after the new year." He hadn't had much of a reason to take vacation time, and the company had been very good about not forcing them to use it during the off time because of the fire.

"Then how about a warm Christmas this year?" JD slowly reached for him, and Fisher leaned over the bed. "I love you," JD whispered. "You're my hero."

"I love you too, but I'm no one's hero."

"Don't be so sure about that. You watched over me and took on someone from your past. You're free to build any kind of life you want, and that's pretty damn heroic in my book." JD had a way of making him feel like he was on top of the world.

"Okay, I'll be your hero if you'll be mine."

"Deal," JD said and pulled him down for a kiss to seal the bargain.

Epilogue

"WOULD YOU calm down and smile a little?" JD asked. "The snow is gone and the sun is out."

"You're just happy because tomorrow morning we're going somewhere warm," Fisher said as he put the last few things in the suitcase and went to close it.

"Stop," JD told him and opened the case again. "We're going to the beach, not the Arctic." He pulled out jeans and two sweatshirts. "You'll need bathing suits, shorts, T-shirts, and something in case it gets cool in the evening, that's going to be about all. It's nearly May, and the sun is going to be bright and the air nice and warm. Think summer, not winter."

"Fine." Fisher added a few more T-shirts. "Are you happy?" He closed the suitcase so JD couldn't fuss any more about what he'd packed.

"We're going to be outside Savannah, so the heat will already have had a chance to start building. It's going to be beautiful, and you're going to have the time of your life."

"I hope I haven't forgotten anything." Fisher knew he always worried about things.

"Then we'll buy what we need. But you are going to have a good time for two whole weeks. My mother wants to come down and see us." JD smiled. "Don't worry—they rented a house nearby for a few days. They aren't staying with us."

JD's relationship with his family had improved a lot over the winter and spring. They'd sold off some of their holdings, and Mary

166

Lynn proclaimed that simplifying their lives was the best thing they'd ever done.

"Good. I like your mother, but I want you to myself." JD's injury had taken a long time to heal, followed by plenty of physical therapy, but that was behind him now. He'd returned to work full-time in late February, and he'd been busy with work and then helping Fisher move in with him last month. Fisher saw JD all the time now, but he still wanted a couple weeks alone with him. JD had promised that his aunt's beach house—well, his beach house now—had a very private back deck, and Fisher was looking forward to getting JD alone on that particular deck and maybe making love under the stars.

There were still portions of the estate to be wrapped up, but the real estate, other than the beach house, had been sold. One of the biggest changes had been that the furniture in their home was now the many family pieces that had been his and JD's aunt's. Their home was filled with warmth and a sense of history and family. Even if Fisher still never heard anything from his own parents.

"What's got you thinking?" JD asked as he sat next to him on their bed. "You get that look every now and then when you're quiet, and I know your mind is turning something over."

"My parents. I think about calling them, but then I don't. They didn't call, not even at Christmas, so why should I bother?" Fisher knew he should simply let all of it go. His mom and dad weren't going to come around, and that was the end of it.

"You know you're better off without them. If they aren't willing to reach out to their son, then they're the ones who are missing out." JD pulled him into a hug. This was the same thing he said each time Fisher brought up his family. At first Fisher thought JD was just saying that, but now he knew he really meant it. The thing was, he'd seen his mother a month ago at the grocery store. He knew she'd seen him, and yet all she'd done was turn away. Fisher had never told JD because he didn't have to. JD was there for him and always had his back.

"Now let me get these bags loaded in the car. Our flight is really early, and I don't want to have to do a bunch of things in the morning." JD hoisted the bags and left the bedroom. Fisher checked his list one more time to make sure he hadn't forgotten anything. He carried the smaller bags down the stairs and placed them near the back door. All he had to get in the morning was the carry-on backpack that JD had given him when he'd gotten him a laptop.

"You know, there's getting to be quite a bit of stuff in the garage," JD said when he returned. "Maybe when we get back, we can look for a way to start that antique shop you've been dreaming of."

"I can't, not yet. I was thinking of starting small. There's an antique show here in November, and I was going to see about getting a booth to try my hand. After that, we'll see, okay?" So much in his life had changed, most importantly his outlook. He didn't worry so much about everything because JD was there to help catch him if he fell. Hell, he knew that JD would always be there to support him if he needed it. What felt best was that JD relied on him to do the same. Being needed had done more than anything to help push back some of his wilder bipolar episodes. He still had them and would for the rest of his life, but they were fewer and further between now.

"You do what will make you happy." JD kissed him right there in the kitchen, holding him tight, the energy between them quickly heating up. He was happy—this made him happy. "I love you," JD whispered.

"And I love you, heart and soul," Fisher whispered right back. He very much felt that the winter, with its snow and ice, was over, and now he was ready for summer.

Did you miss Book One? Check out this excerpt:

Fire and Water

Carlisle Cops: Book 1

By Andrew Grey

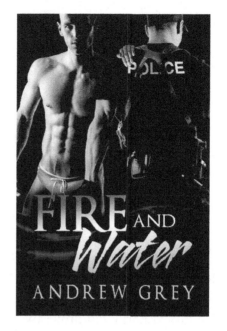

Officer Red Markham knows about the ugly side of life after a car accident left him scarred and his parents dead. His job policing the streets of Carlisle, PA, only adds to the ugliness, and lately, drug overdoses have been on the rise. One afternoon, Red is dispatched to the local Y for a drowning accident involving a child. Arriving on site, he finds the boy rescued by lifeguard Terry Baumgartner. Of course, Red isn't surprised when gorgeous Terry won't give him and his ugly mug the time of day.

Overhearing one of the officers comment about him being shallow opens Terry's eyes. Maybe he isn't as kindhearted as he always thought. His friend Julie suggests he help those less fortunate by delivering food to the elderly. On his route he meets outspoken Margie, a woman who says what's on her mind. Turns out, she's Officer Red's aunt.

Red and Terry's worlds collide as Red tries to track the source of the drugs and protect Terry from an ex-boyfriend who won't take no for an answer. Together they might discover a chance for more than they expected—if they can see beyond what's on the surface.

Available at
www.dreamspinnerpress.com

CHAPTER
One

RED MARKHAM heard the call for backup through the radio, flipped on the flashing lights of his patrol car, and took off down High Street. He turned north and drove two blocks, going through the stop sign as quickly as he could. Red pulled to a stop behind the other squad car and unfolded himself from the seat. He could see over the hood what the problem was and strode over to where two other officers were struggling with a suspect.

"Get the hell away from me. I wasn't doing nothing!" the suspect yelled at the top of his lungs, trying to yank his arm away from Smith. He managed it, too, and used the free hand to punch Rogers. "You have no right!" Smith got hold of him again. The guy wasn't that large, but he was hopped up on something, that was for sure. When Red caught sight of his eyes, they were as big as saucers, red, dilated, and as wild as a feral cat's.

"That's enough!" Red snapped, wielding his voice like a weapon. The suspect continued struggling.

"Tase him, for God's sake," Rogers called. Smith went for his stun gun, but the suspect knocked his hand away. The situation was turning dangerous fast. Red approached and pulled his weapon.

"Get down now!"

The suspect turned toward him and instantly stopped moving.

"I said get down on the ground!" Red's voice became sharper. Drill sergeants could take lessons from him, or so he'd been told.

The suspect's wide eyes got even bigger somehow, and he stilled completely. Then he dropped to the sidewalk on his stomach and didn't move. "What the hell are you?" the suspect asked under his breath.

Red ignored the comment and kept his gun on the guy while the other two officers cuffed him. Once the suspect was under control, Red put away his weapon.

"Jesus Christ, I'm in the middle of the freak patrol."

"That's plenty out of you," Smith told the prone suspect. "You already have more trouble than you can handle." Smith read him his rights and strongly advised him to keep his mouth shut for the foreseeable future. Red stepped back and glared at the suspect, making sure he made no move toward his fellow officers.

"What happened?" Red asked once the suspect was calm.

"Don't know. He looked strange, and when I stopped to see if he needed help, he went off," Rogers explained. He was a few years older than Red, and they'd joined the Carlisle police force at about the same time. Not that Red knew him all that well, outside of work, or Smith, for that matter. Both men were good guys who Red trusted to have his back when he needed it. But calling either of them friends was a stretch.

"The guy's higher than a kite," Smith chimed in.

"Some new stuff has hit town, and it's strong as hell. This is the second guy like this I've had to deal with, and the department's had about six so far. It's bad and getting worse," Rogers added.

The suspect wasn't moving, and Smith bent down. "Shit, call an ambulance. He's barely breathing."

Rogers radioed in, and within a minute they heard sirens approaching. That was the beauty of a town this size. The ambulance garage was only a mile away, and those guys were always on the ball. Red didn't take his eyes off the suspect in case he was playing possum, but he grew more and more limp. The ambulance arrived, and the EMTs took charge of the suspect, worked on him on the ground, and then got him on a gurney and into the ambulance. Rogers rode along, and Smith prepared to follow in their car, but it didn't look good to Red, not at all.

"Hey, man," Smith said just before they got ready to leave. "Appreciate the help." This whole situation had gone from bad to worse to possibly tragic within about two minutes.

"No problem. I'll see you back at the station." The back doors of the ambulance thunked closed, and Smith went to his car. Red waited until they all drove away before going to his. He sat in the driver's seat and adjusted his rearview mirror. He did not look at himself in it. He never looked in a mirror if he could help it. He knew what he looked like and didn't fucking need to be reminded. He was well aware he was never, ever going to win any beauty contests.

Red snapped out of his thoughts when he heard another call—an altercation at the Y. That was a new one. He responded to the call and was informed that an ambulance was already on its way, along with the fire department. What a fucking day. He wondered for two seconds if it was a full moon, but he didn't believe in all that crap anyway, so he flipped on his lights and hurried to his next call.

The Y was in an old school building that had been expanded. The old part was just that, old, while the addition was new, shiny, and well equipped. Red parked near the ambulance and rescue vehicles. He headed inside and was directed to the pool area. Not that he would have had any trouble figuring out where to go from all the people huddled outside the door. People loved to gawk. "Excuse me," Red said, and some of the people turned around. They stared, the way everyone seemed to stare, and silently got out of the way, tapping others on the shoulder, parting groups of people in workout gear and dripping bathing suits like the Red Sea.

Pushing through the door, Red took in the scene. A woman and a young man in a small red bathing suit stood off to the side. The woman, about thirty or so, Red guessed, soccer-mom type, was yelling and trying to poke the kid in the chest. One of the firemen was trying to separate them and looked grateful when Red approached.

"What's going on?" His voice echoed off the walls of the natatorium.

The woman stopped still, and the kid took a step back, nearly falling into the pool. "He...." the woman began, regaining her composure. "He nearly killed my son."

"I did not, lady," the kid protested, crossing his arms over his sculpted chest. Red quickly took him in and swallowed hard. He was a specimen of damn near perfect manhood, like he belonged on the cover of some magazine. He allowed the thought for a split second. "If you'd have been watching your son and making sure he obeyed the rules the way you're supposed to, none of this would have happened."

"All right. You, over there." Red pointed to the kid. "Sit down, and wait for me." Red then turned to the woman. "You, follow me." He took a step back and waited for both of them to obey his instructions.

"Sit here, and I'll be with you in a minute." He waited for her to do as she was told and walked over to where a young boy lay on the tile around the pool. The kid was blue, and Red watched as two EMTs tried to resuscitate him. It didn't look good, but then the kid coughed, spit up water, and gasped for air. Red motioned to the woman, and she hurried over. The boy, who looked about eight, coughed again, and the paramedics told him to stay still. His mother rushed to him, and he began to cry.

"You're going to be all right," the paramedic said to him. Red had crossed paths with Arthur before and knew he knew his stuff. "Just rest and breathe."

"Mom," the kid said.

She took his hand. "You're all right," she soothed, and then she began thanking the people who'd helped her son.

"We're going to take him to the hospital so we can check him out," Arthur told the woman. She nodded and didn't release her son's hand.

"Ma'am, I need to speak with you," Red told her. She nodded and whispered to her son before getting up and walking over to where Red waited. "What happened?"

"I didn't see it. I had dropped Connor off for his swimming lesson, and he was going to stay for open swim afterwards. He and his friends usually do. I got here and saw them pulling him out of the water. I called the police." She turned toward the lifeguard, who sat where Red had told him to. He looked nervous as hell. "I only know that if he'd been doing his job, none of this would have happened," she spat.

Red pulled out his pad and began writing down what she had told him. He got her name, Mary Robinson. He also got her address, telephone number, her date of birth, along with Connor's, and all other pertinent information. "So just to be clear, you didn't see exactly what happened?"

"No, but…." Her argument had rung hollow, and it looked like it was starting to sound that way to her as well. She looked toward her son. Red noticed that she was looking anywhere other than at him. It was something he'd gotten used to.

"It's all right. We'll find out what happened."

She kept looking at her son, and Red stepped back to let her be with him. Then he walked over to where the lifeguard sat on the bottom row of a set of bleachers set up along the side of the pool so spectators could watch races.

Red saw the startled expression on the kid's face as he approached. The kid did a better job than most of covering the pity Red saw flash through his eyes for a split second. "Can you tell me your name, please?" Red asked, getting things moving.

"Terry Baumgartner," he answered, swallowing hard. "He and his friends were horsing around on the pool deck. I told them more than once to stop and was about to ask them to leave when I turned away because a little girl had approached my seat. And when I looked back, I saw him under the water. I dove in, along with Julie." He motioned to the young woman in a red one-piece swimsuit who stood a little ways away. "I reached him first and pulled him out. We started resuscitation right away and continued until we were relieved a few minutes later."

"Who called this in?" Red asked.

A man stepped forward. "I did. They yelled to call 911, so I did. The kids were roughhousing, and I remember thinking someone was going to get hurt."

"Daddy, is Connor going to be okay?" a little girl in a wet bathing suit asked as she walked up and took the man's hand.

"Yes, honey, he's going to be fine," he said, soothing the kid's fears before turning back to Red. He swallowed as he met Red's eyes. Very few people did that anymore. "What he said is the truth. The kids were asking for trouble. If the lifeguard did anything wrong, it was not kicking them out earlier. But he did warn them."

Red glanced to Terry, who nodded. Some of the worry seemed to slip from his aqua eyes, and his godlike, lanky body lost some of its tension. He lowered his lean arms and let them hang down from his sculpted shoulders. Damn—the kid wasn't big, but he was perfect, as far as Red was concerned. "Thank you," Red said, turning back to the man. He took down his contact information and asked a few more questions before thanking him again. He then talked to the other lifeguard, Julie, who confirmed what Terry had told him. Red was satisfied that this was an accident and that the lifeguard hadn't been responsible. He then spoke with the manager of the facility and got the necessary information from him. He was very helpful and seemed concerned and relieved at the same time.

By the time Red was done, Connor had been taken to the hospital, and most everyone else had been dismissed. He was getting ready to leave when he saw Terry and Julie standing off to one side, talking animatedly back and forth. Their voices weren't as quiet as he assumed they meant them to be, because he heard little snippets of their conversation. "I'd die if that happened to me," he heard Terry say and saw the kid looking his way. Red ignored him and walked carefully over the wet tile toward the door. Beauty was only skin deep.

"Red." He turned and saw Arthur approaching. He'd obviously heard what was being said as well. "Don't listen to them. That kid is as shallow as an overturned saucer." Arthur said it a little louder than necessary, and the chatter from the corner ceased abruptly. "When you get off tonight, you want to meet us at Hanover Grille?" he asked more softly. "Some of us are going to have some dinner and hang out for a while. You're welcome to join us, you know that."

Red smiled slightly. He was self-conscious about his smile, and when it threatened to go wider, he put his hand in front of his mouth. "Thanks." His impulse was to say no, thank you, and just go home after work, but Arthur was sincere, and it might be good to get out with people for a change. "Once I'm off shift and get my reports done, I'll try to stop by. It may be late, though."

"I know how things work," Arthur said, and then he hurried away, out of the natatorium.

Red did a mental check that he had spoken to everyone and had all the information he needed. He confirmed he had, and when he checked the clock on the wall, he said a silent thank-you and left the building.

As soon as he pushed open the outside door, he saw four news vans out front, with reporters milling around getting ready to file their stories. Red went right to his car and left, even as they were making their way over. He had no intention of making any comments to the press. He would head back to the station and let the powers that be decide who they wanted to speak for the department.

He got back to the station and filled in the captain about both the suspect on the sidewalk and the near drowning. He made sure the captain knew about the reporters and then headed to his desk to start writing reports. It took an hour. He filed them and got ready to leave. It had been a long, exciting day, and he was exhausted. Red didn't talk much with the other officers in the station. He did say good-bye to the ones he encountered, to be polite, and then hurried to leave.

Red was already in his car and pulling out of the lot when he remembered Arthur's invitation. Since he didn't have anything to do this evening besides sit at home, watch television, and drink too much beer, he decided to take Arthur up on his offer.

ANDREW GREY grew up in western Michigan with a father who loved to tell stories and a mother who loved to read them. Since then he has lived all over the country and traveled throughout the world. He has a master's degree from the University of Wisconsin-Milwaukee and now works full-time on his writing. Andrew's hobbies include collecting antiques, gardening, and leaving his dirty dishes anywhere but in the sink (particularly when writing). He considers himself blessed with an accepting family, fantastic friends, and the world's most supportive and loving husband. Andrew currently lives in beautiful historic Carlisle, Pennsylvania.

E-mail: andrewgrey@comcast.net
Website: www.andrewgreybooks.com

Carlisle Cops: Book 2

Carter Schunk is a dedicated police officer with a difficult past and a big heart. When he's called to a domestic disturbance, he finds a fatally injured woman, and a child, Alex, who is in desperate need of care. Child Services is called, and the last man on earth Carter wants to see walks through the door. Carter had a fling with Donald a year ago and found him as cold as ice since it ended.

Donald (Ice) Ickle has had a hard life he shares with no one, and he's closed his heart to all. It's partly to keep himself from getting hurt and partly the way he deals with a job he's good at, because he does what needs to be done without getting emotionally involved. When he meets Carter again, he maintains his usual distance, but Carter gets under his skin, and against his better judgment, Donald lets Carter guilt him into taking Alex when there isn't other foster care available. Carter even offers to help care for the boy.

Donald has a past he doesn't want to discuss with anyone, least of all Carter, who has his own past he'd just as soon keep to himself. But it's Alex's secrets that could either pull them together or rip them apart—secrets the boy isn't able to tell them and yet could be the key to happiness for all of them.

www.dreamspinnerpress.com

FIRE

AND *Rain*

ANDREW GREY

Carlisle Cops: Book 3

Carter Schunk is a dedicated police officer with a difficult past and a big heart. When he's called to a domestic disturbance, he finds a fatally injured woman, and a child, Alex, who is in desperate need of care. Child Services is called, and the last man on earth Carter wants to see walks through the door. Carter had a fling with Donald a year ago and found him as cold as ice since it ended.

Donald (Ice) Ickle has had a hard life he shares with no one, and he's closed his heart to all. It's partly to keep himself from getting hurt and partly the way he deals with a job he's good at, because he does what needs to be done without getting emotionally involved. When he meets Carter again, he maintains his usual distance, but Carter gets under his skin, and against his better judgment, Donald lets Carter guilt him into taking Alex when there isn't other foster care available. Carter even offers to help care for the boy.

Donald has a past he doesn't want to discuss with anyone, least of all Carter, who has his own past he'd just as soon keep to himself. But it's Alex's secrets that could either pull them together or rip them apart—secrets the boy isn't able to tell them and yet could be the key to happiness for all of them.

www.dreamspinnerpress.com

EYES
ONLY ME
FOR

ANDREW GREY

For years, Clayton Potter's been friends and workout partners with Ronnie. Though Clay is attracted, he's never come on to Ronnie because, let's face it, Ronnie only dates women.

When Clay's father suffers a heart attack, Ronnie, having recently lost his dad, springs into action, driving Clay to the hospital over a hundred miles away. To stay close to Clay's father, the men share a hotel room near the hospital, but after an emotional day, one thing leads to another, and straight-as-an-arrow Ronnie make a proposal that knocks Clay's socks off! Just a little something to take the edge off.

Clay responds in a way he's never considered. After an amazing night together, Clay expects Ronnie to ignore what happened between them and go back to his old life. Ronnie surprises him and seems interested in additional exploration. Though they're friends, Clay suddenly finds it hard to accept the new Ronnie and suspects that Ronnie will return to his old ways. Maybe they both have a thing or two to learn.

www.dreamspinnerpress.com

PATH
NOT
TAKEN

ANDREW GREY

On the train from Lancaster to Philadelphia, Trent runs into Brit, his first love and the first man to break his heart. They've both been through a lot in the years since they parted ways, and as they talk, the old connection tenuously strengthens. Trent finally works up the nerve to call Brit, and their rekindled friendship slowly grows into the possibility for more. But both men are shadowed by their pasts as they explore the path they didn't take the first time. If they can move beyond loss and painful memories, they might find their road leads to a second chance at happiness.

www.dreamspinnerpress.com

THE PRICE

ANDREW GREY

Las Vegas Escorts: Book 1

Hunter Wolf is a highly paid Las Vegas escort with a face and body that have men salivating and paying a great deal for him to fulfill their fantasies. He keeps his own fantasies to himself, not that they matter.

Grant is an elementary-school teacher who works miracles with his summer school students. He discovered his gift while in high school, tutoring Hunter, a fellow student. They meet again when Hunter rescues Grant in a club. Grant doesn't know Hunter is an escort or that they share similarly painful pasts involving family members' substance abuse.

After the meeting, Hunter invites Grant to one of the finest restaurants in Las Vegas. Hunter is charming, sexy, and gracious, and Grant is intrigued. With more in common than they realized, the two men decide to give a relationship a try. At first, Grant believes he can deal with Hunter's profession and accepts that Hunter will be faithful with his heart if not his body. Both men find their feelings run deeper than either imagined. For Grant, it's harder than he thought to accept Hunter's occupation, and Hunter's feelings for Grant now make work nearly impossible. But Hunter's choice of profession comes with a price, which could involve Grant's job and their hearts—a price that might be too high for either of them to pay.

www.dreamspinnerpress.com

Made in the USA
Coppell, TX
03 February 2021